I0713158

Secrets Lost
Secrets Remembered

a novel

MARCIA BREECE

REVISED EDITION

Publishing Partners

Publishing Partners
Port Townsend, WA
www.publishing-partners.com

Copyright © 2013 by Marcia Breece

All rights reserved. No part of this book may be reproduced, stored in, or introduced into a retrieval system, or transmitted in any form, or by any means (electronic, mechanical, photocopying, recording, or otherwise) without the prior written permission of the author.

LCCN: 2012950401
ISBN: 978-1-937454-60-9
eISBN: 978-1-937454-61-6

Typographer: Marsha Slomowitz
Cover Photos: Marcia Breece
Author photo: Winifred Whitfield
Editing: Vicki McCown, Barbara Kindness

dedication

Dedicated to *The Cast And Crew.*
Without them there would be no story to tell.

Other books by Marcia Breece

Finding This Place

Kala's Choice

contents

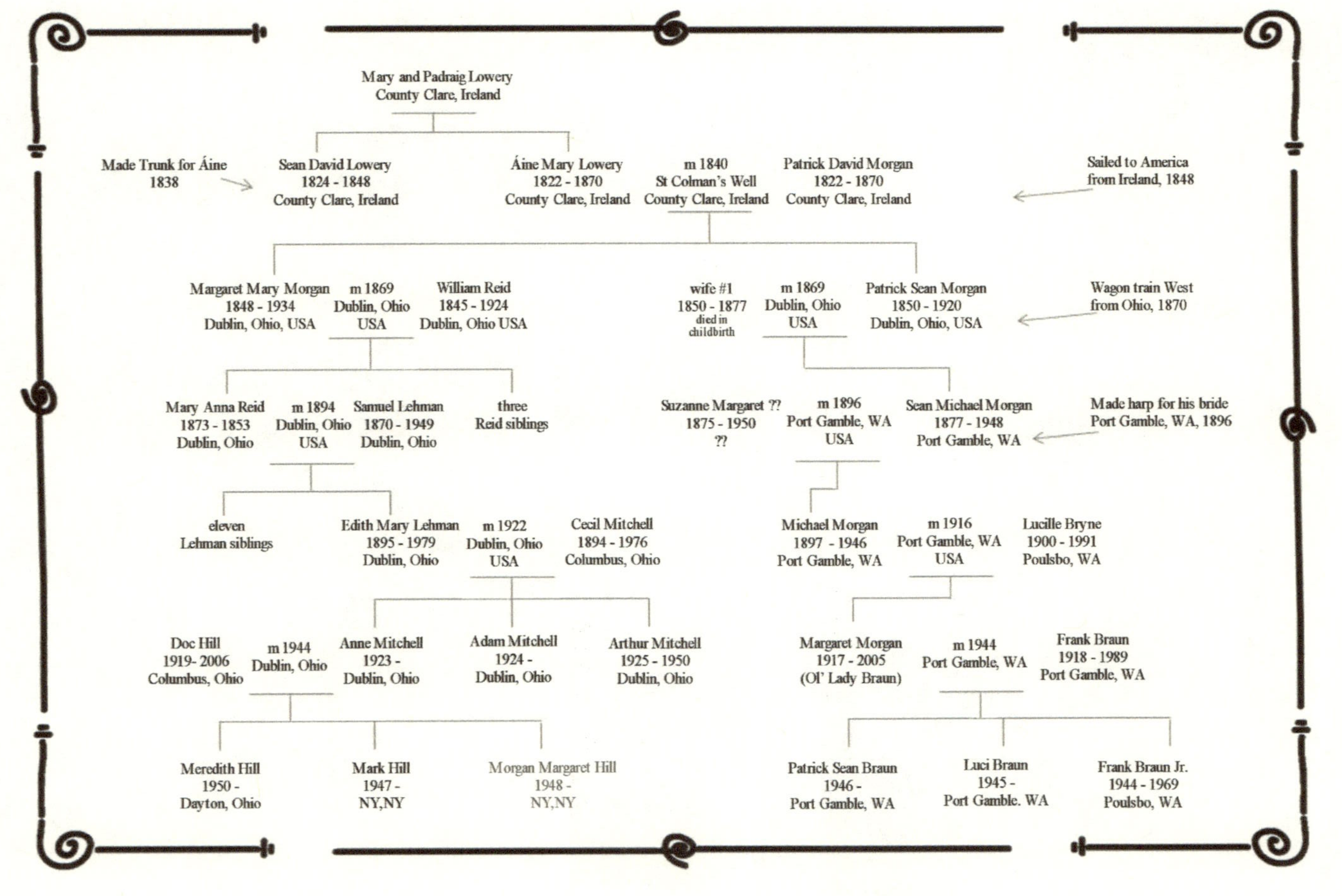

Mary and Padraig Lowery
County Clare, Ireland

Made Trunk for Áine
1838

Sailed to America
from Ireland, 1848

Sean David Lowery
1824 - 1848
County Clare, Ireland

Áine Mary Lowery
1822 - 1870
County Clare, Ireland

m 1840
St Colman's Well
County Clare, Ireland

Patrick David Morgan
1822 - 1870
County Clare, Ireland

Margaret Mary Morgan
1848 - 1934
Dublin, Ohio, USA

m 1869
Dublin, Ohio
USA

William Reid
1845 - 1924
Dublin, Ohio USA

wife #1
1850 - 1877
died in
childbirth

m 1869
Dublin, Ohio
USA

Patrick Sean Morgan
1850 - 1920
Dublin, Ohio, USA

Wagon train West
from Ohio, 1870

Mary Anna Reid
1873 - 1853
Dublin, Ohio

m 1894
Dublin, Ohio
USA

Samuel Lehman
1870 - 1949
Dublin, Ohio

three
Reid siblings

Suzanne Margaret ??
1875 - 1950
??

m 1896
Port Gamble, WA
USA

Sean Michael Morgan
1877 - 1948
Port Gamble, WA

Made harp for his bride
Port Gamble, WA, 1896

eleven
Lehman siblings

Edith Mary Lehman
1895 - 1979
Dublin, Ohio

m 1922
Dublin, Ohio
USA

Cecil Mitchell
1894 - 1976
Columbus, Ohio

Michael Morgan
1897 - 1946
Port Gamble, WA

m 1916
Port Gamble, WA
USA

Lucille Bryne
1900 - 1991
Poulsbo, WA

Doc Hill
1919- 2006
Columbus, Ohio

m 1944
Dublin, Ohio

Anne Mitchell
1923 -
Dublin, Ohio

Adam Mitchell
1924 -
Dublin, Ohio

Arthur Mitchell
1925 - 1950
Dublin, Ohio

Margaret Morgan
1917 - 2005
(Ol' Lady Braun)

m 1944
Port Gamble, WA

Frank Braun
1918 - 1989
Port Gamble, WA

Meredith Hill
1950 -
Dayton, Ohio

Mark Hill
1947 -
NY,NY

Morgan Margaret Hill
1948 -
NY,NY

Patrick Sean Braun
1946 -
Port Gamble, WA

Luci Braun
1945 -
Port Gamble. WA

Frank Braun Jr.
1944 - 1969
Poulsbo, WA

gratitude

Thanks to my dear actor friends, Kimberly King and Ken Grantham, for helping this book materialize. They endured single-minded dinner conversations and character-sharing long before the story developed. They offered feedback and provided sanity checks as I progressed. I am grateful for their patience and support.

Thanks also to my friend, Heidi Jack, who loaned me her tapes and books and patiently read the manuscript—twice—before it was ready for the world to see.

Sounds True became a source of knowledge and background through their diverse metaphysical and spiritual selections. I'm grateful for the introduction to new teachers as well as the opportunity to listen to hours of free interviews.

Thank you to Sarajane Williams for providing background music from *Harp Music for Healing* for the book trailer, not to mention my continued enjoyment of her beautiful music.

I am grateful for the work of many teachers: Wayne Dyer, Dee Wallace, Jennifer McLean's *Healing with the Masters*, Eckhart Tolle, Byron Katie, Deepak Chopra, Bruce Lipton, Deanna Fulton, Gregg Braden, Christy Whitman, Hay House Radio, Shifra Hendrie's, Sonia Coquette, Doreen Virtue, Panache Desai, Shakti Gawain, Barbara Marx Hubbard, and many more.

Beta readers included Rich Nevin, Chuck and Gretchen Howard, Elizabeth Warren, Kathleen Toomey, and Susan Sleek, whose feedback helped make the story flow.

Thanks also to my editor, Vicki McCown. Some people have skills and some people have talent Vicki is blessed with both. I'm grateful for her involvement and encouragement.

chapter one – the healers

FOR THOUSANDS OF YEARS ONLY Healers walked the caves, safe, warm and well-fed deep in their catacombs, communing in their monastery of native consciousness as hibernating bears, digesting the year's experience. Their language had no word for *ownership* but included fifty words for *light*, and even more for *love*. All needs were met. They thrived, stress-free. Fear did not exist. Each Healer maintained his or her energetic balance.

In winter, surface temperatures dropped below zero and Arctic winds blew. Ice crystals covered the frozen earth as quartz crystals formed in bottomless exothermal pools below the healers' living quarters. In summer, they hauled the warm, curative waters to the surface to nourish the crops and feed the nomads' cattle.

Soon, self-contraction and separateness would invade their sanctuary and drive human enlightenment into deep slumber for more than two thousand years.

chapter two – the trunk

*The intuitive mind is a sacred gift
and the rational mind is a faithful
servant. We have created a society
that honors the servant and has
forgotten the gift.*

—Albert Einstein

"THIS TRUNK SEEMED SO MYSTERIOUS in Grandma's attic," Morgan told her mother. "I remember following her up those narrow steps. I must have been five or six that summer. While Grandma Edith rubbed oil into the leather, I played dress-up with dusty lace curtains, big-feathered hats, and high-heeled shoes..." Morgan inhaled the memory, then with the shake of her head and a quick blink, returned to her mother's living room.

"I brought it home after Mom died, your Grandma Edith," Anne said, as if Morgan didn't know. "There's not much inside—some photos and an old quilt. I saw a camelback trunk on that show—you know, the one where people bring in their antiques and get them appraised? Well, that one was worth several hundred dollars, so I thought I'd see what I could get for this at her estate sale. But then, for some reason… I don't know why exactly… I just couldn't let a stranger take it. Maybe you can use it to store extra blankets when you get settled in Seattle."

"Where'd Grandma get it?" Morgan asked.

"Your great-great-great-grandmother, Áine Mary Morgan[1], brought it to America from Ireland. We've named the women in our family after her for generations: my mother, Edith Mary; her mother, Mary Anna; her mother, Margaret Mary; and me, Anne. I gave you Áine Mary's last name first, of course." Anne slowly closed the trunk. "Patrick, Áine's hoodlum husband, chose exile to America over hard labor. Apparently he stole food during the Irish potato famine. They settled in Dublin, Ohio. That's where I was born."

By the time Morgan's mother inherited the trunk, no one remembered....

Áine's ancestors had abandoned their Celtic traditions to become Catholic while Patrick's family attended the tiny Church of England. The light that glowed between Áine and Patrick held neither designation.

Áine Mary Lowery and Patrick David Morgan were married outdoors in County Clare. On their wedding day, Áine's mother carried buckets of water from St. Colman's Well, which she heated over a fire. Áine stepped into the tub of warm sacred water to wash her red hair and thin, young body. Patrick's mother carried water for her son's nuptial bath as well. When Áine and Patrick vowed a lifetime together, however, their purity far exceeded the cleanliness that came from bathing.

For the wedding, Áine's family dressed in their finest clothing, a year in the making. After the men sheared the sheep, Áine's mother and grandmother cleaned and carded the wool, then spun the yarn and wove heavy fabric, using beets, roots, and berries to dye the wool with colors of the earth. The wool for Áine's dress was left un-dyed and bleached in the sun.

On the wedding day, Áine, her parents, and her brother, Sean, walked over the rocky hill from the north toward St. Colman's Well. Áine wore a dress made of finely spun, tightly woven natural wool, the color of the

---

1   **Áine** *(awnya) - means radiance in Gaelic, an Irish form of Anne. In Irish mythology, Áine is the queen of the fairies, a goddess of love, and growth. Rites in her honor involve fire and the blessing of the land. The feast of Midsummer Night was also held in her honor.*

clouds in the sky. Below a braided halo of lavender, wildflowers, and white ribbons, her long red curls moved with the breeze.

Since jumping rocks as children in the fields between their homes in County Clare, Áine and Patrick knew they were destined to spend their lives together. As in previous lifetimes, they would support each other in whatever came their way.

Standing in the little stream flowing from St. Colman's Well, Patrick and Áine promised to love and take care of each other forever. Like liquid silver, the cool sacred water poured over their bare feet. Only Áine's mother saw the luminescent rainbow materialize between Áine and Patrick, as it connected like an unbroken circle, mirrored in the silvery spring water.

After the wedding, the couple retreated to a cottage not far from Áine's childhood home. Inside they found her trousseau, including the trunk Sean had made for his sister's sixteenth birthday. Four years before, Sean had hewn precious boards from a huge oak limb, then covered the trunk's exterior with sheepskin he tanned and tooled with Celtic knots and spirals. On the back, near the bottom, he carved:

S.D.L. ~ 1838.

On the wedding day, Áine's mother placed a note on top of the trunk, written on paper she made from pulp.

MAY THIS TRUNK HOLD MANY LIFETIMES OF HAPPY MEMORIES

Inside, Áine found a wedding quilt stitched by her neighbors and friends and a soft yellow blanket knitted from milkweed silk.

The year before the wedding, Áine's mother had gathered milkweed pods and spun the silky fiber into fine yarn. She made yellow dye from yarrow then knitted the soft blanket, hoping that someday it would swaddle Áine and Patrick's firstborn child.

Each morning, after their wedding, Áine and Patrick carried water from St. Colman's Well to their little cottage for washing, cooking, and gardening.

While Patrick worked in the field, Áine sat in a rocking chair by the fire, mending a shirt. She heard a timid knock at the door. Placing her round-framed spectacles on the table, she answered the door.

A noise like the barking of a terrified seal echoing on the Cliffs of Kilkee, rose from a tiny bundle. "I'm sorry to bother you, miss," said a gaunt, frightened woman. "My baby has a dreadful cough. I've heard tell of your special healing powers. Please... can you help my baby?"

Áine invited them into her cozy cottage, served sweet tea to the woman, and rocked the sick infant in her arms. Laying the baby on the warm rug by the fire, she removed the blanket, stained sienna with filth, revealing the sunken, feverish face of a baby girl. Áine whispered a prayer. "Divine Mother-Father-Universe, bless this infant and her mother and restore good health to both so this baby might live to offer her gifts to the world."

When Áine rubbed her palms together and held them over the malnourished infant, an amber glow filled the shadowy cottage. She continued her prayer as she bathed the infant with warm well water. When she opened her trunk to get the yellow baby blanket, the scent of sweet wild flowers and earth wafted to the ceiling like ocean mist in a sunbeam. Rocking the swaddled infant in one arm, Áine ladled hearty soup from a pot hanging near the fire, then hummed a lullaby until the mother finished the only food she'd had in days.

Áine positioned the infant back in her mother's arms. The baby girl eagerly nursed while Áine stood behind, both hands on the mother's shoulders, imbuing life force energy that would strengthen both mother and infant.

"How can I thank you?" asked the revived young mother. "You saved my baby girl."

The mother bent to retrieve the dirty rags and began to remove the special golden blanket.

"The blanket is my gift. It will keep her safe and warm," Áine said in the woman's unique Gaelic dialect.

"You are too kind," the mother said. "I will call her Órga[2] and remember you always," and she disappeared into the damp winter afternoon.

Áine closed the door against the cold air and tossed the dirty rags into the fire. She said another silent prayer for the woman and her infant daughter as she put on her glasses and returned to mending.

While Ireland starved, Patrick's garden grew an abundance of vegetables, more than their families could eat. Patrick shared his produce, and Áine tended to the needs of strangers who came to their door. Soon villagers, both Catholic and Protestant, became skeptical of the newlyweds' intentions. Fearful of their mysterious powers, the villagers forced Áine and Patrick out of Ireland. With their belongings packed in the oak-and-leather trunk, Áine and Patrick Morgan boarded a ship to America and eventually settled in Ohio. They called their village Dublin.

Morgan rested her palm on the trunk's lid. "I'm glad you didn't sell it Mom," she said.

The next week, Morgan left Ohio to follow her career to Seattle and the trunk came along with her household goods. The heirloom waited at the foot of her bed for twenty more years. She knew the trunk's value exceeded its age, artistry, and exceptional condition; however, being a single mother building an executive career left no time for nostalgia.

---

2   **Órga** – *golden light*

chapter three – lavender

Try looking at tomorrow, not yesterday,
and all the things you left behind…
In these days of nameless faces,
there's no one truth, but only pieces
My life is all I have to give.
Dare to live!

—Andrea Bocelli, *Vivere*

LURED BY A SUNNY FALL WEEKEND and a longing her career could never satisfy, Morgan Hill took a ferry across Puget Sound. Munching a still-warm cinnamon roll, she toured the Poulsbo Farmers Market, filling a fabric grocery bag with crisp green beans, fresh-dug potatoes, and lacy-topped carrots.

A baseball cap secured her thick blonde hair and Bocelli's *Vivere* spilled from the sunroof as she cruised winding country roads, trying to elude the discontent that plagued her.

Cresting a hill, she slowed. Drawn by an old farmhouse, she pulled to the side of the road. Cattails circled a misty pond beyond the house while cedar trees and overgrown perennial flowerbeds framed an unbroken view of the Olympic Mountains. A huge Oregon maple shaded the south side of the house while the driveway curved under a mammoth Douglas Fir near the road. Llamas grazed in its shadow. *That tree must be hundreds of years old,* she thought. *I wish it could tell me its story.*

If she could hear, the texture of its timber would tell the story of her own ancestors, descendants of Áine and Patrick Morgan. Their son, Patrick Sean Morgan along with his bride, drove a wagon across the plains and through the mountain passes. They started not far from Morgan's hometown in Ohio and homesteaded what became this estate. The Douglas fir would tell of grazing cattle sold in Port Gamble to feed lumber mill workers and Percheron horses working in well-trained unison, pulling the wagon full of logs to the mill. The same team heaved the stumps, their massive hooves digging into the rich soil as they prepared the land for pastures, crops, and gardens.

Someday Morgan would learn that this property had supported her ancestors for generations, the tree a silent observer.

She noticed the *For Sale* sign and impulsively called the listing agent from her cell phone. Within weeks, Morgan sold her elegant Seattle condominium for a handsome profit, retired from her fast-paced international career, and purchased Ol' Lady Braun's five-acre estate, complete with the five llamas. She made plans to open a bed and breakfast.

With her usual zeal, she threw herself into developing a business strategy and marketing plan. She researched and purchased reservation software, selected a color palette, designed a logo, and created a website that would tempt guests to the peaceful, upscale inn. She named her business Morgan Hill Retreat and spent the rainy winter months directing renovations. She hired a contractor to update the kitchen, add a bathroom, paint all the rooms and build coops for chickens and waterfowl. The makeover took a big bite out of her savings account, but she counted on an increase in value over the next few years, ultimately increasing her investment.

During that first winter, Morgan ignored the pungent scent of paint, the gritty taste of drywall dust, and the disturbing wail of a demolition saw while she googled the culinary and craft applications of lavender. Then she rented a rototiller, guided the jerking and roaring machine to prepare a wide strip of rich earth near the western fence line, and planted assorted varieties in rows to produce layers of fragrant lavender.

In April, Morgan booked her first B&B guests as Ol' Lady Braun's perennial beds revealed creamy-yellow hybrid peonies, delicate red-and-white bleeding hearts, and pointed purple lupines mixed with emerging Shasta daisies.

By late June, lavender buds in graduated shades of purple set a striking backdrop for the outdoor weddings she hosted at the inn. Her overnight guests picked bouquets to take home, and she made sachets and lavender wands to sell in her gift shop at the top of the stairs.

chapter four — doc's dead

*Memory is one of the most beautiful
realities of the soul. Since the body itself
is so linked into the visual sense, it often
does not recognize memory as the place
where the past is gathered. The most
powerful image of a memory is a tree.*

—John O'Donohue

"Hɪ, Mᴏ." Mᴏʀɢᴀɴ's ʙʀᴏᴛʜᴇʀ, Mᴀʀᴋ, born a year before her, called her *Mo* before he could say any other word. His voice sounded softer than usual and she knew. "Doc died last night."

For as long as she could remember, they had called their father *Doc*, just like everyone else in the small Ohio town where they grew up. It suited him far better than Daddy or Dad.

"Thanks for letting me know... I'm sorry I didn't make it over there... before." Despite her indifference toward their father, she felt a twinge of guilt for not helping Mark.

"Don't feel guilty about that." Mark said. "Doc hasn't recognized anyone for a while now, and he was still as nasty as ever. He treated me like crap every time I went up there. It didn't matter if he knew me or not."

"Do you need me to do anything, call people, anything?" she offered.

"Thanks, but I have everything under control. He made me his executor a couple years ago, and I've had power of attorney since I moved him out from Ohio into the retirement home." Actually, Mark had moved their father to three different facilities north of Seattle. The old man's cantankerous attitude got him thrown out of the first two.

"Do you need help going through his things?"

"They will give his clothes to charity, that's about all there is. He put the furniture, photos, and antiques in a storage unit when he and Mom divorced. When I moved him from Ohio to the retirement community, he told me he didn't need any of that crap, but he wouldn't tell me where the unit was." Mark took a deep breath. "Then I found the bill he hadn't paid and I called the storage place back in Ohio. He quit paying so they sold everything. Sorry I didn't tell you before. Nothing we could do about it anyway."

"Even Grandma Hill's antiques?" Their father had inherited his parents' furniture, photo albums, and German china. Doc had taken everything after the divorce from Morgan's mother.

"Yep, sold to strangers," said Mark. "Most fathers would want their kids to have stuff like that, but Doc couldn't care less."

"Wow, true to character all the way to the end.... Are you sure you don't need my help?" she offered again.

"His friends are dead. I'm sure you don't want to fly to Ohio to organize a memorial service any more than I do. I'll put his obituary in the paper there, and send one to his alma mater in New York."

"Mark, I appreciate all you've done. You were so patient with him. I don't know how you did it."

"I always thought that eventually...I don't know...he'd wake up or something." Mark was just beginning to allow the pain of their childhood to seep into his consciousness. He would deal with memories of their abusive father in his own way, just as Morgan had done, years before.

"I'm planning a dinner, just the immediate family. I assume you'll be too busy with the B&B."

"You know he's been out of my life for a long time and Mer...," her voice trailed off. They had often discussed how uncomfortable they both felt in the same room with their sister Meredith.

"I can't cancel bookings. This is my first season, I have bills to pay, and frankly, I've grown beyond the need to participate in Meredith's drama just because I'm her sister." Morgan took a breath. Even thinking about Meredith seemed to suffocate her. "Maybe you can come to the farm and help me plant a tree in Doc's memory..."

"He always liked dogwood trees..." Mark's voice was still and faded even further into not-so-fond memories of Doc.

"Mark, call me if you want to talk. Even if I have guests coming and going, I'll be here if you need me."

Morgan sat on the bench under the big maple and waited for the grief. Nothing came. She couldn't remember a time in her life when she felt her parents' love. They taught her the opposite of love; indifference, still she wanted to do something to mark the end of his life. *Where's the best spot to plant a dogwood?* she thought as she looked around the farm.

The next day, the wind blew unusually strong for a sunny July first. She lost her hat under the big maple while pulling weeds among the shade-loving hellebores, big-leafed hostas, and bright-red impatiens.

"Come on, Howard, I'm hungry." Morgan named her puppy Howard. She found the company of the Bichon Frisé far more rewarding than his human male counterparts. He eagerly ate whatever she served, patiently waited in the car when she ran errands, and happily followed her anywhere.

As she pulled leftover chicken and lettuce from the refrigerator, a loud crack rippled through the air and the house trembled. At first she thought they'd had an earthquake.

"Oh my lord," she said aloud, looking out the kitchen window. The high wind had split the maple. Half of the tree stood garishly splayed, with a woodpecker's nest exposed to the wind, no longer cradled at the vortex of the double trunk. The other half had smashed the corner of the back porch. Green leaves the size of 33 LPs and brown mossy branches blocked the back door. It had bounced between the dormers above the garage, taking the gutters with it. Huge limbs had crushed Morgan's cherished BMW.

She flew into action, first calling her homeowner's insurance company. The agent didn't have time to inspect the damage until after the Fourth of July weekend. "Just take lots of pictures and email them to me, then go ahead and have the debris removed."

Grateful that the tree missed the expensive satellite dish that provided the inn's high-speed Internet service, she found a local tree service on line, then called her auto insurance agent. He arrived within the hour.

"The car's totaled; there isn't a spot that isn't bent or broken. Nice car. What year was it?" That word, *was*, sent a shudder of grief through Morgan as the insurance agent thumbed through the pages on a clipboard.

"A 1995 BMW 528i…, I drove it for eleven years."

"Do you know the mileage?"

"It just turned past 199,000, but it still looked like new. I remember thinking that my car would turn over 200,000… about the time I turned sixty." She forgot about the agent standing there as she leaned on the car with both hands. "I took such good care of it… all the scheduled maintenance… never had a problem…."

She loved that car. She'd paid cash for it after the India assignment. Writing a check for a luxury car made her feel successful—valid—real.

Morgan felt as if the tree had smashed her success along with her car.

Before opening the inn in April, she shot images of the house, maple tree, and spring garden, which she used on her web site and printed brochure. Photography had been her passion since she was five years old. Now, she hurriedly shot without enthusiasm before Kevin's Tree Service arrived at 4:00 p.m.

They cut the heavy trunk and bulky branches off the porch and car, and silenced the chainsaw before the guest arrived at six.

After breakfast the next day, as Kevin's Tree Service returned to fell the remainder of the tree, her neighbor, Mr. Wakefield, walked up Morgan's driveway.

"Bad luck there. It's a shame 'bout yer car. Too bad it wasn't parked in the garage."

"Yeah, organizing the garage wasn't a priority when I was getting this place going. Guess it should've been. The insurance company will pay for a rental car for ten days. I have guests coming for the weekend and bookings every day until the end of August. When am I going to have time to shop for a new car?" It was a rhetorical question.

"What ya need here's a pickup truck."

"You're probably right," Morgan said, not really paying attention.

"Tell ya what, I been teachin' my grandson to be a mechanic. He's been workin' on a classic ol' truck I found. It's only got 30,000 miles on it."

Now he had Morgan's attention.

"We're pretty much finished rebuildin' it."

"You mean the red one parked in your barn? You'll sell it?"

"That's the one. It's a 1955 Chevy. Ya s'pose a thousand'd be too much? The body's perfect and the interior's like new. An ol' lady down there on Big Valley Road kept it in her garage after her husband died of a heart attack in 1956. Come on over. You can drive it around for a while and see if ya like it. You mind drivin' a stick?"

"Not at all. I drove a Subaru with a standard a long time ago. Maybe you can give me a refresher. I'll come over tomorrow after I serve break-fast, if that's okay. Thanks, Mr. Wakefield. By the way, do you want any of this maple for firewood?"

"Naw, I got plenty a firewood. I'll send my grandson over ta split 'n' stack it fer ya. Ya can pay 'im whatever ya want. He needs money to put gas in that fancy new truck he bought."

"Great, send him over." Although the inn didn't have a wood-burning fireplace, Morgan occasionally used the fire pit in the private area behind the house. *This will be enough for a lifetime of fires,* she thought.

Morgan felt the tree's lingering spirit as she watched the chainsaw attack the maple's garishly exposed timber. A shudder rippled through her slender body as a cloud of sawdust blew across the yard like a ghost on Halloween. The house shook when the last living portion crashed to earth between the porch and the fence. All the air squeezed out of Morgan's lungs as the old tree's energy swirled like heat on desert sand. Trying to catch her breath, she looked up at the Douglas fir by the driveway. Though the air was still, its branches moved, as if the ancient tree waved goodbye to its one-hundred-year-old friend. She cried, then sobbed when she realized the death of the maple had created a feeling of loss far greater than the loss of her eighty-seven-year-old father.

"After we pull the stump, I'll plant a new tree for you, ma'am," offered Kevin. "Insurance usually covers replacement in cases like this."

Embarrassed, Morgan wiped her cheeks with both hands. "Thank you, Kevin. How about the biggest dogwood you can find?"

chapter five – biz visits

To meet everything and everyone
through stillness instead of mental noise
is the greatest gift you can offer
to the universe.

—Eckhart Tolle

BIZ STEPPED FROM HER CONVERTIBLE. Her long gray ponytail swung free as she tossed her hat onto the white leather seat. "I love your new farm!"

"And I love your new car!" said Morgan, smiling down from the wrap-around porch.

Biz patted the hood of her baby-blue BMW Z4, then pointed to the garden beside the house. "The dogwood is gorgeous. Is that where you lost the big maple you told me about on the phone?"

Morgan nodded.

Behind her, rough-sawn western red cedar siding wrapped the exterior of the farmhouse. In the late 1940s, Ol' Lady Braun's husband felled cedars, clearing space for their house and barn, opening the view of the Olympic Mountains. The knotted wavy edges of hand-milled cedar dipped and curved around the house like sand in the surf. Morgan wondered if the scent of cedar came from the weathered siding, the remaining trees, or a distant memory.

"The place is beautiful," Biz said, "but what possessed you to buy a farm in the middle of nowhere?"

"Probably the same demon that made you buy a baby blue sports car," said Morgan. "I'll be sixty soon. I need to change while there's still time."

Morgan and Biz had met twenty years before when Morgan became the director of marketing at a wireless telecom company and hired Biz's advertising agency to do marketing communications. At work, Morgan called her Elizabeth, but out of the office, she became Biz. Both women were single and intensely serious about their careers. Together they enjoyed big salaries, fancy restaurants, high-end spas, and fancy cars.

"Let's go to lunch. I'm starved," said Morgan, leaning over the railing. Then with a sarcastic grin beneath the bill of her baseball cap, she asked, "Shall we take my truck or your convertible?"

With a shriek, Biz pointed at the red truck parked by the garage. "You replaced your BMW with that old pickup truck?" she said with thinly veiled condescension.

Not surprised by Biz's reaction, Morgan said, "My car was eleven years old when the tree fell on it, so I didn't get much from the insurance company and I only had ten days to find a new vehicle. Anyway, I always wanted a red pickup truck. I think it's cute." She knew Biz enjoyed the BMW's esteemed reputation, and not just its efficient dynamics and luxurious comfort. Although Morgan grieved for her luxury car, her practical side knew the truck met her needs.

Biz rolled her eyes and shook her head with a laugh. "Let's take the convertible...unless you need to stop for hay or something."

Morgan leaped down the porch steps like a much younger woman to catch Biz in a hug. "I'll show you the inn after we eat," Morgan said as she folded her long legs into the passenger seat.

"Don't you want to put on makeup and change clothes?" asked Biz, noticing the holes in Morgan's jeans.

"Biz, this is Kitsap County. No one cares what I wear, and neither do I. What freedom." She threw her arms into the air. "I love it here!"

At Burratas Bistro, Morgan ordered a glass of the Pinot gris.

"Water please, it's a little early for wine," said Biz.

So many rules, Morgan thought, as she put her hat on the empty chair beside her, allowing her thick curly hair to spring into natural streaks of copper, silver, and gold.

"What happened to your hair? You were blonde the last time I saw you."

"I quit abusing it," said Morgan.

"You've gone granola! Wild red hair. No makeup. Socks and Birkenstocks. The pickup truck…" Biz laid down her menu and leaned forward, scrutinizing Morgan. "The new 'do suits you though. You look like a red-headed Carole King."

"Why, thank you. Might as well let my hair go natural like the rest of my life."

At that, the two spontaneously burst into a few bars of "You Make Me Feel Like a Natural Woman," then laughed, happy to be the only mid-afternoon patrons.

"I could have built a school in Africa with the money I spent keeping my hair smooth and blonde for all those years," said Morgan, "not to mention the mani-pedis."

"All the time we've hung out, I had no idea you were a redhead."

"Me either, until I stopped the abuse. I wore a hat for six months while it grew out. My hair was sort of strawberry blonde when I was a kid, then turned muddy when Maggie was born. After the divorce I had it foiled and straightened and never stopped," Morgan said.

Morgan sipped her wine and looked across at her friend. They had lived parallel lives in both social and business environments. They infiltrated the good-old-boys corporate club and won from the inside, both aware of the sacrifices necessary to achieve equal pay for more than equal work. Biz still battled. Morgan's consciousness, like her wiry curls, remained ironed flat throughout their friendship—her creativity, feminine vigor, and intuitive powers nearly obliterated. Morgan wondered if her friend would understand the reclamation of her wild feminine Self.

"This salmon is fabulous." Biz closed her eyes and savored her meal. "And the green beans… yummm! I had no idea Poulsbo had a restaurant like this."

Morgan tried not to bristle at Biz's condescending attitude. "Biz, you might be surprised what you'll find in a place like Kitsap County," she said.

They enjoyed their late lunch/early dinner in the small Norwegian tourist town, then cruised tree-lined winding roads, passing horses in white-fenced pastures, grazing in the late-day sunshine.

"You never know what the weather will be like in the Pacific Northwest. Today's perfect for driving with the top down.... Ahhh, that wine really relaxed me," Morgan said, gathering the fall air with both hands stretched overhead and her head pressed against the headrest.

"I love driving this car on winding country roads," said Biz, "and I always have the top down unless it's pouring rain."

"I have to admit, I miss my car. I can feel how this holds the road."

"Ruth loves driving a sports car too. She's borrowed it so many times, I think she's filled the tank more than I have," said Biz.

Biz's sister Ruth was a close friend of Morgan's. A year younger than Biz, a little taller and just as thin, Ruth majored in philosophy and minored in music, then married Tom a week after graduation. She taught piano and violin lessons while staying at home with their two children. Now Tom Jr. had a medical practice in Santa Fe and her daughter, Sarah, the same age as Morgan's daughter, was a partner in a Seattle law firm.

Biz tolerated Ruth's tarot readings and ignored most of the paranormal topics Ruth liked to discuss. Biz didn't believe in past lives or metaphysical events. You're born, you live, you die.

"Next time, Ruth should come along. Tom can live without her for a day or two," said Morgan.

"Ruth would love your farm," Biz agreed. "Tom would love it too. They should book a romantic weekend sometime."

As they drove back to the farm, Morgan looked over at Biz enjoying the wheel of her sports car. Morgan wondered if her friendship with Biz could survive now that Morgan's life had changed so drastically. Only time could tell.

Morgan took two stemless glasses from the cupboard. "Red or white?"

"White."

She poured cold Pinot gris and put the bottle back into the fridge. After a quick tour of the guest rooms and Morgan's private space over the garage, they settled in the living room below the cathedral ceiling.

"Sorry to hear about your father," Biz said. "How was the service?"

"I guess they had a family get-together. At eighty-seven, he'd outlived all of his friends. I didn't go." Morgan kicked off her Birkenstock sandals, peeled off her gray socks, and looked down at her callused feet. Unlike Biz, she no longer had money for manicures and pedicures. "One of these days, I've got to work on these feet. Running around barefoot all summer was really hard on 'em," she said, avoiding the conversation about her father.

Howard jumped onto the chair, turned around by her thigh, and then fell asleep with his chin on her knee.

"You didn't go?" The evening sun at her back made Biz's long hair look more blonde than gray as she leaned over to untie her Stuart Weitzman espadrilles. She placed them neatly by the old trunk, sat on the sofa, and propped her perfectly pedicured toes on the coffee table.

"That's right. I didn't go."

"Isn't that disrespectful of your father, even if you weren't close?" said Biz.

"I don't think he noticed," Morgan said in a low voice as she took a sip of wine. She leaned to the side, avoiding the evening sun in her face.

"What about your mom, brother, and sister?" Biz continued. "Don't you want to support each other?"

"Mom divorced him thirteen years ago, while I was in India, then she moved to Bellingham to be close to my sister. She'll miss him even less than I will, if that's possible."

"You never told me they divorced. How long were they married?"

"Forty-nine years. I called it *The-End-of-the-Long-War*."

Biz looked shocked, and wondered why she knew so little about Morgan's family.

"No surprise to anyone who knew them." Morgan had rarely discussed deeply personal issues, even with her closest friends, but now, as she opened to a more authentic life, she shared her past with Biz. "I guess Mom figured nearly fifty years of being treated badly was long enough. For as long as I can remember, they never liked each other. Anyway, if I went to the funeral, my sister would be there judging my behavior, and trying to fix us all. The usual mêlée."

"When was the last time you saw your sister? What's her name? Mary Beth?" Biz asked.

"Meredith, a combination of two family names, Mary and Edith. She dropped by one afternoon when I first moved in, then started a fight about our father's hospice care."

Morgan's sister Meredith had arrived at the farm unannounced just after their father moved to the third retirement community. Morgan was kneeling in her new flowerbed, removing rocks and preparing the earth for lavender plants when the big black Mercedes passed the llamas.

"What are you planting?" asked Meredith, walking across the lawn. The cold breeze tossed her wavy blonde hair around her flawless, fair-skinned face. Tall and slender, she was still as beautiful as the day she left Ohio to study ballet in Paris. She never danced professionally but she still carried herself with deceptive elegance and grace.

"All kinds of lavender," said Morgan as she rose to her feet, giving her sister an air hug. "Sorry, I'm all muddy." Howard sat behind Morgan and, uncharacteristically, made no effort to great the guest.

Although Mark and Morgan called their father Doc, Meredith always called him Daddy, even as she grew older. "I came to see your new place and talk about Daddy's care." Meredith said, answering Morgan's unspoken question.

"Now?" said Morgan, brushing the dirt from her knees before removing her gardening gloves. Wet Northwest winters offered rare occasions for planting and Morgan had hoped to finish the lavender bed before the rains started again.

"Well, I think it's important, even if you don't," snipped Meredith as she turned toward the house, expecting Morgan to follow. "I called from the ferry, didn't you get my message?"

"No, I've been working in the garden most of the day." Morgan quickened her pace, catching up with her sister. "Come inside, I'll show you the house and make some tea."

"I'll get my bag."

"You're spending the night?"

"Of course, it's a B&B isn't it?"

'Not yet', she wanted to say but swallowed—hard. "Sure. I'll make up one of the beds…."

After a tour of the unfinished rooms, Morgan said, "Let's sit on the porch. I'm too muddy to sit inside."

"But it's breezy on the porch," whined Meredith.

"Is the kitchen acceptable?"

Meredith rolled her eyes, and sat on a kitchen chair, waiting for Morgan to serve her tea. "I'm taking Daddy for an MRI next week," she said.

Morgan poured Insta-Hot water over tea bags in big red mugs. She gave one to her sister, then leaned against the kitchen counter. "The last time I talked to Mark he said Doc doesn't know anyone most of the time, and even when he does, he's miserable. What will an MRI tell you besides that he's eighty-seven years old, almost deaf, nearly blind, and has cancer of the liver?"

"I can't just sit around and watch him die. I've got to do something."

"I think we should just keep him as comfortable as possible and let nature take its course. I know for sure this isn't the life he'd want." Morgan blew into her mug, then sipped her tea. "Why spend time and money on tests that can't possibly change his quality of life?"

"How can you be so awful to Daddy? You are such a bitch, I don't even like you!" As if a sudden shape-shift transformed her, Meredith stood up and punched Morgan in the mouth. Turning on her platform heel, she grabbed her Louis Vuitton duffel and stomped out, leaving the front door wide open.

Morgan heard tires spinning in the gravel driveway as she found an ice cube to soothe her swelling lip.

It wasn't the first time Meredith hit Morgan. Meredith often flew into a rage, even with less provocation. Every time, she seemed to forget and joined family events acting sticky-sweet as if nothing had happened.

Remembering the confrontation, Morgan took a big gulp of wine. "It's not that I don't like my sister," she told Biz. "I'm not comfortable with my Self when I'm around her. Bottom line—I didn't go to a service I don't believe in, with toxic people, for a man who didn't love me or any of his children, especially his daughters."

"You really think he didn't love you?"

"Love is for Hollywood movies and Hallmark cards. I'm not sure I even know what the term means, but I'm sure he didn't like being a father. God only knows why he had three children. I've always participated in family events out of obligation, not out of love. I won't do it anymore. Going to his funeral would have been a lie."

Biz didn't know what to say. She was close to her family and couldn't fathom what Morgan had lived through.

"You know," Morgan said, "I think my father will be nicer to me now that he's dead."

Biz laughed. "You think he'll be back—like a ghost?" Then she realized Morgan wasn't smiling.

"Not like the ones in movies with muddy hands coming out of cemetery dirt and charred body parts falling like autumn leaves." Uncharacteristically open about her secret thoughts, Morgan leaned back and looked up at the cedar ceiling in her huge living room, trying to select her words carefully. "Spirits maybe? I don't know what I believe—but I don't think we really go anywhere, the *real* us." She patted her chest and felt her heart beating faster than usual. "Maybe our spirits just keep hanging around after the body's finished." Morgan shrugged her shoulders and wrinkled one side of her mouth. "Maybe there are layers of reality, like channels on the TV, or radio frequency, but we can't see because we don't understand."

"That's ridiculous," Biz grunted.

"Remember when Ruth saw your mother in the garden picking flowers after the funeral?"

"That was just Ruth's grief causing a mirage," Biz insisted.

"Didn't the three of us talk about guardian angels one time?"

"Ruth believes in all that stuff. I never bought into it. Anyway, that's about religion, not dead people."

"I'm not so sure. How can we ever know?" Morgan said.

"We can't." Biz escaped to the kitchen and opened the fridge. "You want more wine?"

"Sure, why not? We're not driving anywhere," said Morgan.

Biz and Morgan sipped their wine and watched orange and fuchsia streak behind the Olympic Mountains, as if the sunset could provide insight. The wine delivered the abandon Morgan needed to share her emerging ideas.

"Maybe our spirits preselect our time here on the planet for some reason or purpose. I wonder how many times we come back to find the experience we need. Maybe my siblings and I chose our parents so we could learn from each other. Am I obligated to allow my sister's abuse and negativity just because we were born to the same parents?"

Biz came from a kind, demonstrative family. She and her sister Ruth spent a lot of time together, going to the movies, shopping, and socializing with the same people, including Morgan.

"My family isn't like yours, Biz. I have a brother I adore and enjoy spending time with but my sister's negative energy irritates me like static on the radio. How can I love them equally? I don't think chromosomes and DNA mandate love. We share parents and an unpleasant childhood, that's it." Morgan walked to the window and spoke as if gates to her past had opened. "I think Meredith got the worst of Doc's rage. I learned to be sort of invisible to stay off his radar, but she always tried to get her own way—even when he was drunk and out of control. I guess each of us had to learn our own lessons. I try to respect Meredith's choices, but that doesn't mean I need to spend time with her. We're taught that we should love our families. Maybe in caveman days, humans without a family unit were vulnerable. I feel more vulnerable with my family." She ran her fingers through her wiry curls and settled back into the leather chair. "I think my nomadic lifestyle helped me find my Self."

Listening quietly, Biz began to realize why she knew so little about Morgan's family and childhood. She eased to the new topic of conversation. "Your promotion to the international department happened about the time I opened the Denver office. We both got so busy, we lost touch for a couple of years. You wrote to me from Hong Kong—weird—that was before email. I forget, where did you work after Hong Kong?"

Morgan gazed at the big round lamp behind Biz, remembering her twentieth-floor suite at the New World Harbour View, over ten years before.

A spherical lamp stood weirdly positioned, away from the end of the sofa. Every night she moved the lamp away from the window to open the view of the harbor, and every day the maids moved it back. That's when Morgan learned about feng shui; the practice of arranging furniture so that energy or chi could flow gently and smoothly. The properly placed lamp prevented unwanted energy from flying into the room. At that point in her life, Morgan just wanted an uninterrupted view of the lights of Kowloon reflected on the harbor.

By the time she bought the farm, however, she found feng shui more interesting. She bought a book Altared Space: Harnessing Healing Energy Using Feng Shui Principles *by Nicholas Cappele, then tried to follow the principles to decorate her bed and breakfast. She placed a sofa between the front door and the fireplace next to a round end table and spherical metal lamp to deflect 'the dragon's cosmic breath.' She unpacked the carved wooden dragon she bought in China—long before she'd heard of feng shui—and placed it on the desk by the stairs to guard check-ins and harmonize the space. Following suggestions in the book, she hung a water-like mirror across from the front door to draw in good energy and a small, om-tuned wind chime on the porch to protect the outside.*

"After Hong Kong I went to London, Australia, and India— more escape than career choice. I was trying to find my own energy."

Morgan's use of the word *energy* made Biz uncomfortable. She sipped her wine and ignored it.

"For example," Morgan went on, "the Hindus believe that they must stay in the caste they're born into until their next incarnation. Many of them don't even try to have a better life because they don't believe it's possible in this lifetime."

"Do they still have arranged marriages in India?" said Biz.

"If I were born in India, my father would've sold me at birth." Morgan stared at the sunset. "I read somewhere that about ninety percent of marriages are arranged. Can you imagine meeting your husband for the first time on your wedding day?"

"No, I can't imagine! Even as little girls, though, our mom taught Ruth and me that we'd become half of a couple. We never considered having a career and taking care of ourselves until much later. Ruth's lucky; she and Tom love each other. I spent years in bad relationships and searched as if my happiness and well-being depended on finding a mate." Biz took a big gulp of wine, washing away the taste of her own past. "I tried to conform to the couple mentality and dated men that were *so* wrong for me, even married one because I thought I *should* be married."

"Isn't that odd, I never knew you were married." Morgan realized that her friendship with Biz had been one-dimensional, like the rest of her life for the past fifty-plus years. In their efforts to excel in the male-dominated business world, Biz and Morgan had both denied their feminine power, leaving deeply personal thoughts and belief systems out of their conversations, as most men did.

"I'm glad you never met that jerk," said Biz.

"Have you ever met a woman over fifty who started her adult life believing she could do anything she wanted? That she was smart enough, strong enough, worthy enough?"

"Besides Ruth? Maybe one or two," Biz said. "Ruth is one of the few women I know who has the courage to be who she is. She ignored all that women's lib stuff in the seventies, stayed home to raise her kids, and dances to her own tune, literally."

＊

Biz's sister Ruth was born old and wise. Her feminine power remained intact and she instinctively understood the healing powers of melody, harmony, and silence. At age three, she created cheerful, buoyant tunes with her grandfather's old fiddle. The music lived deep inside her long before she learned to read the notes. She began lessons on a miniature French violin her father bought when she was only four years old. When little Ruth drew the bow across the strings, the air around her filled with love and gratitude. Her music resonated in the hearts of nearby grown-ups and caused joyful tears to rise up from deep in each listener's soul. As an adult, Ruth offered her talent to children whose parents respected and supported the rhapsody of music. Teaching music to children was not Ruth's profession as much as her calling.

⌁

"Humans went off track somewhere," Morgan told Biz. "A goose doesn't speculate about his purpose on the planet. Many animal fathers in the wild abandon their mates as soon as the female is pregnant, when the male has served his purpose of procreation. My father was as indifferent to his family as any father could be—more lion than human."

"Geese mate for life, don't they?" Biz said.

Morgan laughed despite her bad humor. "Yes they do. Still, if there's another female in the barnyard…" She laughed aloud, "…the gander will nail her!"

"Wow—how'd we get off on this stuff? You didn't go to the funeral. Tomorrow, let's go shopping in Port Townsend!"

"Sorry I'm in such a bad mood tonight. Shopping won't help. I don't have an income until I get more bookings, and I spent a lot renovating this place. Let's go for a hike on Hurricane Ridge. It's beautiful up there." Morgan pointed to the trunk. "In the morning, will you help me carry that trunk to the little attic above the landing?"

"Sure, we can do that before we leave for Hurricane Ridge. What's in it?" Biz said over her shoulder as she went to the kitchen to get them each a glass of water.

Morgan followed. "There's a quilt and some photos. Sounds odd but I haven't looked inside since I left Ohio. It sat in Grandma's attic when I was a kid…. It's not that heavy."

Her fingertips brushed the trunk's camelback lid as she passed.

chapter six – through the glasses

*Every extension of knowledge arises
from making conscious the unconscious.*
—Friedrich Nietzsche

HAVING SURVIVED HER FIRST HECTIC SUMMER as an inn keeper, Morgan settled into the white rocking chair with a mug of hot coffee and Howard draped over her knee. His chin rested on her freckled arm. Weekend guests had checked out, leaving the inn vacant until Friday. She relished the solitude.

The base of the Douglas fir by the driveway measured more than five feet in diameter. Owning an old-growth fir tree and the surrounding property seemed peculiar to Morgan. She felt like a treasured visitor; more caretaker than owner.

Breathing the fresh fall air, and savoring the deep sense of belonging, Morgan ignored inn keeping duties. Just over the ridge, Hood Canal flowed beyond her sight and the Olympic Mountains stood hidden in the clouds. Still, she felt them. She sipped coffee and watched a bald eagle stretch his talons toward a branch of the Douglas fir. "Sorry, chicken isn't on the breakfast menu," she said aloud as if the eagle would understand. Provoked by his attack on a rooster, Morgan had covered the area around the coop with netting to protect her treasured chickens.

Standing between the house and road, the gambrel-roofed barn, also built with hand-hewn second-growth timbers, offered shelter for the five llamas that once belonged to Ol' Lady Braun. Looking strange against her memory of black and white Holsteins, the serene long-necked creatures preferred grazing in the gentle rain. The tranquil scene reminded Morgan of childhood days on her grandparents' dairy farm. Homesickness covered her like a warm cozy blanket.

With surprising urgency, she found herself taking two stairs at a time toward the landing above the living room. At the top, she stretched to pull the red-handled rope, and the attic stairs unfolded. Roof beams kept the world at bay while Grandma's trunk and its contents lingered like a world traveler waiting for repatriation.

Kneeling on the attic floor, Morgan's fingertips traced the Celtic knots and spirals tooled in the trunk's leather exterior. Vague memories of innocence and awe glistened like hazy liquid crystal. When she lifted the heavy lid, ancient memories rose into the rafters like mist reflecting the morning sun. The quiet scent of earth and wildflowers filled the dimly lit space.

Blue light through the round gable window illuminated the inside where a drawing of a young woman in a heavy floor-length gown told the story of women's fashions when Áine Mary Morgan boarded the ship to America in 1848. *Why did I wait so long to explore this?* she thought, unaware that it had taken years of silent preparation.

Only now could she begin to understand the secrets concealed inside, as if opening a portal to memories from another life.

Morgan touched a tattered quilt and remembered her grandmother's words, *My mother and her friends hand-stitched each patch and gave it to Cecil and me for a wedding gift.* Great-Grandma Mary Anna cut rectangles from scratchy work shirts and cumbersome dresses that had come to the end of their usefulness, then lovingly hand-stitched each to the next in a brickwork pattern that reminded Morgan of piano keys.

Each patch of fabric told its own story: the red plaid wool worn by Great-Granddad as he hitched his team of horses to plow Ohio cornfields; the mauve velvet dress worn by Great-Grandma as she played the piano before the birth of her first child, Edith Mary; the white-on-white cotton christening gown worn by baby Edith and each of the eleven siblings who followed.

Morgan touched her heart and felt the contrast between the buttery softness of her polar fleece shirt and the quilt's scratchy wool patches. As she moved the quilt aside, she noticed letters embroidered on a blue dungaree rectangle.

CUIMHNIGH

With both hands, she gently placed the quilt on the floor next to her, wondering who *Cuimhnigh* might have been.

An Art Deco eyeglass case waited among the photos. The sage-green leather case squeaked softly, liberating a pair of round-rimmed spectacles. Thickly packed light suddenly filled the room. Morgan's heart raced beneath her pale-yellow shirt. *I drank too much coffee this morning,* she thought.

She pulled herself to her feet and walked to the small round window, the glasses gently balanced in her palm. Dark clouds filled the sky and rain pounded the driveway far below the attic. Lars, the male llama, stood watching the storm from the safety of the barn, the female llamas kushed[3] in the shadows behind him.

Trying to ignore the faint, mysterious light in the room, she placed the glasses on the quilt and continued to explore. Loose inside a leather album she found a familiar sepia image. Grandma Edith, stood with her husband, Cecil; her mother Mary Anna; and all eleven brothers and sisters. Mary Anna held Anne, Cecil and Edith's first-born child, who appeared to be about six months old. *This must have been taken in the summer of 1924. My mother was Mary Anna's first grandchild.* Morgan thought. In the photo, Edith wore glasses like the ones Morgan found in the trunk.

As naturally as taking her contemporary reading glasses from her purse, Morgan removed the antiquated pair from their case. After gently cleaning the lenses with her shirttail, she positioned the metal stems behind her ears, then shivered as if cold electrical current penetrated her skin.

Memories unfolded…

---

3   **kush** - *The term for the act of a llama laying down or the actual position a llama is in when it is laying down.*

Three-year-old Morgan walked a tractor-rutted path with her great-grandmother, Mary Anna. Their heather-green hand-knitted sweaters matched and so did their hazel eyes. Morgan's mother struggled to catch up, with Meredith toddling beside her. Morgan's four-year-old brother, Mark, tried to run ahead but Mary Anna shooed them back to the house.

"You go on back now. Let me be with my great-granddaughter, and don't worry, I'm more than able to walk to the woods," she said in her heavy brogue. Although born on a farm in Ohio in 1873, she still spoke with her parents' Irish accent.

Like steel and redwood shavings, curls escaped Mary Anna's loosely twisted bun while the breeze teased strawberry wisps from Morgan's ponytail. She took Mary Anna's bumpy, spotted hand as they crossed the pasture, avoiding the Holsteins. Morgan used both hands to help her great-grandmother cross the shallow stream by the woods. Their shoes got wet. Neither noticed. In the autumn glow of maple and oak, Mary Anna found the widest old stump and sat down. Morgan climbed up, scratching her knee on the rough bark. Her damp sneakers dangled from the edge as they sat for several minutes, listening to woodpeckers and blue jays.

"Do you see the light there darlin'?" Mary Anna asked while gently rubbing Morgan's scuffed knee with her bony, parchment-covered hand.

"Purple?" said little Morgan. They watched semi luminous orbs float among the trees while the hazy purple glow danced to peaceful, crystalline tones of Irish clàrsach[4] and Russian balalaika[5].

As generations before her, Mary Anna's healing powers remained secret most of her long, hard life. Giving birth to twelve children and helping her husband farm their land left no time for contemplation and discovery. As they sat on the stump, she knew that years would pass before Morgan

---

4   **clàrsach** - *the generic Gaelic word for 'a harp.' In English, the word refers to a small Irish harp.*

5   **balalaika** - *a musical instrument with a triangular body and three strings, popular in Russia.*

remembered the music she heard that light-filled afternoon, but she had so little time to pass along her knowledge.

"Yes, yonder there." Mary Anna pointed toward the dense center of the woods with her cane. "You're born a special girl, Morgan Margaret Hill. You'll be seeing the colors your brother and sister can't see."

"Mark and Sister went to the house with Mommy." Morgan snuggled close and rested her cheek on the old woman's knee as weary fingers coiled Morgan's soft curls.

Mary Anna's gaunt, crone face smiled down at Morgan's cheek. "Even if they'd be with us here, they wouldn't be seeing the colors. Dear one, there is so much you must learn." As if she continued in her ancestors' Gaelic language, Great-Grandma's brogue-laden voice drifted through the woods. "At times, you will be confused by the emotions of others seeping into your body like spilled milk into a sponge. This happens to all humans, but unlike others, your gifts will cause these feelings to amplify, resulting in profound emotions you won't recognize. Their origin will confuse you. Just remember that these out-of-place feelings don't belong to you. Don't allow them to overtake your body. If you stay focused on who you are, they will vanish."

"The body has non-physical centers, as vital to well-being as the heart, eyes, and lungs. Just as your heart knows to beat, it also knows to love. The centers will help you sense your world. They connect your physical body to non-physical parts of your Self. This is true for all humans. Someday, because of your special ability, you will discover how your intent relates to these centers and you will help others understand."

As the words flowed, Great-Grandma Mary Anna knew this would be her only opportunity to share what she knew with Morgan. "Most importantly, live with intent. Concentrate on positive aspects of life. You will attract matching vibrations and draw to you what you focus on. If you want to be happy, you will be happy. If you think about being sick, you will be sick. This is the most important knowledge I can teach you.

"You are too young to comprehend my words; however, some part of you will remember. Someday you will meet a wise young man who will *lead you on the journey of our ancestors. Until then, know that I will always be nearby when you need me."*

Her words floated over Morgan's head but found quiescent consign deep in Morgan's memory. Although Morgan could not comprehend the meaning, she understood that her great-grandmother loved her deeply.

A year later, Mary Anna died in her sleep. While the grown-ups attended the service, the neighbors, Mr. and Mrs. Dupper, looked after the children. Mrs. Dupper rocked Meredith in the porch swing, while Mr. Dupper took Morgan and Mark on a walk to the woods. The children ran as fast as they could across the pasture ahead of the helpful neighbor and, as always, got their feet wet maneuvering over the rocks in the creek. Morgan found a seat on the same old stump while Mark climbed a nearby cottonwood. She heard the faint music of ancient string instruments as a rose-colored orb danced close by.

"Hi, Grandma Mary Anna."

Mark laughed and so did Mr. Dupper.

"Poor little ninnyhammer. Your great-grandma's gone. She's not here anymore," said Mr. Dupper.

"Yes... but..."

"Nin-ny-ham-mer, Nin-ny-ham-mer, Nin-ny-ham-mer," Mark teased.

Morgan pointed to the rose-colored light. Mark and Mr. Dupper saw only the trees.

"We best be gettin' back to the house. It looks like a big storm's a-brewin'."

Mark's blonde head bounced over the rolling pasture while thunder-clouds darkened the western sky. Morgan stayed on the stump until Mr. Dupper insisted, "Little lady, we'll be struck by lightnin' if we don't get across that field before the storm comes."

With a wrinkled brow and curls falling over serious eyes, four-year-old Morgan glared at the neighbor man. She jumped off the stump and looked up at the glowing rose-colored light.

"Bye-bye, Grandma."

Morgan's memory of the colors and the music faded.

Lightning flashed and thunder clapped and the llamas retreated deeper into the shadowy barn. As Morgan turned back to the attic, a ball of rose-colored light appeared and began to move around the attic. A harp-like hum in her ears lingered long after the thunder. *Like music among the trees,* she thought as the faint memory emerged.

Remember, Remember, Remember echoed in her mind like a happy jingle. She closed her eyes, tilted her head back, and listened to the blissful string melody. Her heart swelled with a sense of love she hadn't experienced in fifty-five years. Wearing the glasses, Morgan felt strangely calmed by the dense, colorful orbs that joined the rose-colored light. She sat by the trunk, rolled back to rest her head on the quilt, and watched the lights gently move like floating swans among the rafters. Slowly, as they danced to odd-sounding tunes, she began to understand that this was only the beginning of her spiritual journey. A powerful sense of gratitude caused tears to trickle into her thick hair, a feeling more intense than the electrical storm still raging beyond the roof.

From that day forward, the old spectacles replaced her contemporary glasses, causing previously invisible layers of life to appear all around her. She began to see the complexities of human life in a very new way.

Suddenly seized by the need to know the meaning of the letters stitched into the quilt, she hurried down the folding stairs to her office, nearly stepping on Howard waiting at the bottom. She googled the letters: C-U-I-M-H-N-I-G-H, discovering it was a Gaelic word meaning *remember*.

chapter seven – anne's visit

*Every human being's essential nature
is perfect and faultless; after years of
immersion in the world we easily forget
our roots and take on a counterfeit
nature.*

—Lao-Tzu

"I'M COMING TO SEE YOUR B&B ON MONDAY, after my water-aerobics class at the gym," Anne said. More active than most forty-somethings and as fiercely independent as a four-year-old, Morgan's mother lived in a condominium in Bellingham not far from Morgan's sister, Meredith. "You don't have guests do you?"

"No, Mother, I don't have guests booked until the weekend. Things are slowing down now that the high-season is over. It's a good time for you to see the place."

"You'll need to give me directions," Anne said.

"If you're driving from Bellingham, you'll need to take the Edmonds ferry to Kingston. The dock is about fifteen minutes from my farm." She waited for the information to sink in. "I have a better idea. Meredith could drop you off at the train station, and I could meet you in Edmonds. Amtrak stops right at the ferry dock. That would be a more relaxing trip for you."

Morgan met Anne as she disembarked in Edmonds, then they rode the ferry to Kingston where Morgan had parked the truck. "You replaced that fancy car with this old truck?" her tone of voice shredding Morgan's serene life like an out-of-tune ukulele.

"Yes, Mother, for now it's more practical."

As they drove into Morgan's driveway, Anne said, "Why on earth would you want llamas? Can't you find a new home for them?"

With a tickle in her throat, Morgan replied, "They add ambience for the B&B, and their fiber is softer than sheep's wool. The woman who lived here before sold her cattle and raised llamas because she loved to spin and weave. Her daughter left a big bag of yarn for me. You know how I knit while I watch movies. I made some hats and scarves for my gift shop upstairs and I sell the yarn. It's a little extra revenue."

"How often do you have to shear them?"

"Every spring, like sheep."

"Sounds like too much work," Anne said with a pinched face.

"It's all part of my back-to-nature phase I guess. Anyway, I've grown rather fond of them, especially Lars, the black-and-white one." Morgan took her mother on a tour of the house and Anne decided to sleep in the Sunflower Suite, the biggest and most expensive room in the inn.

"This room is beautiful, and so spacious. I love the little breakfast table in the sitting room. You actually did a good job, it's not all cluttered with doilies and trinkets like most B&Bs."

Thinking, *Don't sound so surprised*, Morgan said, "It's my favorite room as well. I thought about moving my things in here and letting guests have the rooms over the garage except that I can charge more for this space, and I need the income."

"I like the yellow matelassé coverlet and the sunflowers on the garden gate headboard. Where did you get it?"

"That's why I call this the 'Sunflower Suite.' I bought the iron gates at a store in Georgetown and the four-by-fours were in the barn. I stained them to match the doors and hired a carpenter to build the frame." She put her mother's bag in the dressing area and made a ceremony of opening the French doors to the porch, as she did for all her guests. "You'll see the Toulouse geese out here in the morning when I let them out of the coop. They're fun to watch."

"You have domestic geese?"

"Yes. When I moved in, I bought baby chicks, Indian Runner ducklings and a pair of Toulouse goslings. They all stayed in a pen in the garage under a heat lamp until the contractor finished the two coops.

Now they're grown up and laying eggs. The Runner ducks are very entertaining and the geese add a sense of grace, floating on the pond."

"You don't serve your guests the goose and duck eggs do you?"

Morgan ignored her mother's revulsion. "Duck eggs are great for baking and so are the goose eggs. I don't like them scrambled though."

Over scrambled chicken eggs and coffee the next morning, Morgan wanted to ease into a conversation about the glasses. She wondered if Anne had any knowledge of their powers. When Morgan pulled the glasses out of her frizzled red curls, Anne said, "What happened to your hair? It used to be so pretty when you kept it blonde and straight. Is that part of your back-to-nature thing too?"

Morgan knew, even as a little girl, that her natural hair was ugly. She remembered her mother's harsh words as she roughly brushed the tangles, *"It's too bad you got your great-grandmother's frizzy red hair and not soft blonde waves like your sister."* As a young woman, Anne's blonde hair fell into smooth waves. Now, gray blended with the blonde, still shiny, soft, and beautiful.

Suddenly, Morgan erupted in a fit of coughing as if she choked on something foul.

"Are you getting a cold?" her mother asked.

"No, I feel fine," she croaked. "I think it's the cedar pollen." Thinking, *it's not pollen season.*

"I noticed your old-fashioned reading glasses, like the ones my mother wore in the twenties. They look like you found them in the glove box of that old truck. Certainly you can afford glasses that are more… stylish."

"I like the retro look," Morgan said with a cough. "I found them in Grandma's trunk. The one you gave me before I left Ohio."

Before Morgan could mention the unusual phenomenon caused by the glasses, a knowing glance swept over Anne's face, and she rose to her feet remarkably fast considering her age. "I need to wash some delicates. Do you have any Woolite?" she asked in a harsh, don't-ask-questions tone of voice.

"Of course. It's in the cabinet in the laundry room. Do you want my help?" Thinking, *You just got here yesterday.*

"No, no, I'll find it," she said with an emotionless, blank face and hurried out of the kitchen.

A few minutes later, she came back and sat down to finish her coffee.

"Let's take Howard for a walk in the tree farm, the weather's lovely," Morgan suggested.

"Oh, I didn't bring the right shoes for walking in the mud."

It hasn't rained for weeks, Morgan thought. "Then let's go for a ride. I'll show you our little town and we can walk the beach at Point No Point."

"In that truck?" Anne groaned. "Are you serious?"

"Okay Mother, what *do* you want to do?" Morgan said. Unable to get her breath, she burst into a coughing fit.

"I think you better just sit and rest. You're catching a cold."

Morgan gave up trying to entertain her mother. Anne spent her time at the farm knitting and watching TV while Morgan vacuumed and re-set an upstairs guest room, tended to her animals, mowed the yard, and prepared their meals.

Convinced that Morgan had a sore throat, Anne said, "Seems like every time I visit, you get sick. You should see a doctor about that cough."

Morgan didn't understand that she allowed her mother to restrict her ability to speak her own truth. She felt as if a leather belt were cinched around her throat. Soon, Morgan would learn how the throat chakra embodies communication.

On Thursday morning, they rode the ferry to Edmonds—drinking lattés, discussing recipes, and watching sea gulls float on the wind behind the boat. Morgan kept the conversation as prosaic as possible. Once Anne boarded the train to Bellingham, Morgan rode the ferry back to her old red truck parked in Kingston and drove to her new life, away from Anne's criticism, judgment, and narrow perspective.

As Morgan prepared the Sunflower Suite for weekend guests, the coughing quieted. She knew the tickle in her throat had nothing to do with cedar pollen. She felt choked whenever Anne interrupted and disapproved. Communicating with her mother was impossible.

chapter eight —
meeting patrick braun

Thousands of candles can be lit from a single candle, and the life of the candle will not be shortened. Happiness never decreases by being shared.

—Buddha

Suddenly, Howard stood up and looked at Morgan.

"You need to go outside?" she said, as she closed a book.

Rather than running to the back door, Howard sat down.

That's not it. "Well, what do you want then? You ate your dinner an hour ago."

His black eyes floated upward as if watching steam rise from her hair. Then with an adorable cock of his head, he looked her in the eye again. Without thinking, Morgan touched the back of her head, then turned toward the kitchen.

"Howard! What are you looking at?" His eyes drifted again as he twisted his head. "You're very cute when you do that, but I have no idea what you want."

As she opened the book, something near the kitchen caught her eye. Wearing the glasses, she stood and walked towards the window wondering if a car had pulled into the driveway. Just then, a greenish translucent orb floated past her and vanished near the back door. Its energy felt angry and sad, but nonthreatening.

Over the next few days, the faint greenish light appeared in the pasture when she fed the llamas and again when she read a book on the porch while her washer and dryer labored. She thought that oddly reflected light could have caused the faint green glow.

One Friday afternoon around 2:00 p.m., a beat-up Chevy Malibu pulled into the driveway. A man and woman climbed the front steps. They turned to admire the Olympic Mountain view before ringing the doorbell. Their auras were quite separate and their tentative body language indicated they were friends but probably not lovers that would be sharing a room for the weekend.

Morgan pushed the glasses into her hair as usual and answered the door.

"Hi, I'm Patrick Braun," the man said apologetically. "This is my friend Cathy Buchannan. Hope we're not disturbing you."

"Hi, Patrick, Cathy. Come on in. Do you have a reservation?"

"Oh, no. We were just driving around, reminiscing, and something made me stop here. Cathy and I dated in high school, and she just moved back to Poulsbo." His words flowed in a nervous rush, like a teenage boy on a first date. "I grew up on this farm and I haven't been back up here since Dad died. His name was Frank Braun. You bought the place from my sister, Luci. Would you mind if we looked around the farm? I helped my dad dig the pond with a big green bulldozer. He had a terrible time keeping that old thing running. Guess that's where I learned to be a mechanic." Patrick finally took a breath.

"Sure, look around all you want. Would you like to see the inside too? I've converted the house into a bed and breakfast. In fact, I thought you might be tonight's guests arriving early."

"Are you sure you don't mind?" asked Cathy. "We're happy to just walk around outside."

"I don't mind at all." Morgan looked at Patrick. "Which room was yours?" When he pointed to the top of the stairs, she said, "Go on up and have a look. Really, it's fine. I have people in and out all the time. I'll stay here, read my book, and wait for my guests. Just make yourselves at home."

"Thanks, we won't be long," Cathy said as they left their shoes by the front door.

Morgan heard them walking around upstairs, talking softly. "Look, she added a bathroom next to my old room," Patrick whispered.

"This is charming, I love the colors." As they came back down, Cathy said to Morgan, "Where did you get the beautiful photographs?"

"They're mine. I've been a photography nut all my life and I travelled all over the world."

"You've done a beautiful job here. It feels open but private, very nice," said Cathy.

"Thank you." Morgan followed Cathy and Patrick onto the porch. As they put on their shoes, she said, "You're welcome to hang out in the barn and walk around outside. Just be sure to keep the gates closed."

"Dad raised cattle when we lived here. I know all about keeping gates closed."

"We had bonfires in the pasture over there," Cathy added, pointing westward. "It's great to see the place again. Thanks for being so gracious."

"I'm glad I was home." Then to Patrick, "Before you go… do you mind telling me a little about your parents? When did they buy this property?"

"My mother inherited several hundred acres from her family who homesteaded here in the late 1800s or maybe early 1900s, I have no idea exactly when. Dad and Mom kept the surrounding one hundred acres and sold the rest after Mom's dad died." Patrick put his hands in his pockets and looked toward the mountains. "I remember Mom telling me how they cut down a bunch of second-growth cedars to open up the view and clear a place for this house and the barn. They took the logs to the mill in Port Gamble. The beams, studs, and siding for the house and barn came from those trees. That was in the early 1940s, before I was born. You know, even though he was never what you'd call happy, Dad loved this place." Patrick shook his head, "Seemed like he wasn't happy unless he was angry."

"I'm familiar with that syndrome," said Morgan. "Do you know the name of the people who homesteaded the property?"

"My mother's maiden name was Morgan and my great-great-grandfather's name was Sean Patrick. Guess that's why Mom named me

Patrick Sean. Sure glad she didn't name me Sean Braun," he laughed with a snort.

Morgan's face flushed. Patrick looked at her curiously. "Sorry…" she said, rubbing her cheeks. "It's just that… I'm named after my great-great-great-grandparents, Áine and Patrick Morgan. They had a son named Sean but they settled in Ohio… from Ireland."

"Wow, what'r the odds?" Patrick said, as he bent to tie his shoes.

"Funny how similar the names are," said Cathy. Patrick Braun headed for the pasture, not the least bit moved by the suggestion that he and Morgan could possibly be distant cousins.

Morgan leaned against the railing as a blue RAV4 turned into the driveway. "That must be tonight's guests. Hang out as long as you like," she told Cathy. "It's a beautiful afternoon for reminiscing."

After showing the guests to the Sunflower Suite, Morgan settled into the rocking chair on the wrap-around porch and pulled the glasses from her hair again, ready to go back to reading. As she waved to Cathy and Patrick getting into his old Chevy, she noticed a green light glowing brightly in the back seat.

She looked down at Howard draped over her knee and raised one eyebrow as shivers rippled down her back. She whispered, "Do you think that green orb might have been Frank Braun?" Howard's plume-like tail swished as he jumped from her lap. "Let's go for a walk in the tree farm," she said, leaving her book on the chair.

They crossed the road and ducked beneath cedar branches heading into the Christmas tree farm. Well-established red cedar, alder, and Oregon maple lined the path they walked almost daily. The madrona trees reminded her that Hood Canal's salt water flowed just three miles away, far from her native Ohio woods. Every time Morgan walked the trails of the hundred-acre property, she remembered Great-Grandma Mary Anna, her grandparents' dairy farm, and their woods filled with oak, maple, cottonwood, and ash.

chapter nine –
mrs. doctor thomas

*Why do you stay in prison when
the door is so wide open?*

—Rumi, *The Essential Rumi*

During Morgan's second season of operation, a travel agent called to follow up on a booking. "When Dr. and Mrs. Thomas arrive tomorrow, they'll need both Merlot and Chardonnay. Are you aware that Merlot should be served at room temperature and Chardonnay should be chilled?"

Morgan tried to be polite. "Yes ma'am. I drink a little wine now and then. There is a small refrigerator in the room. I'll chill the Chardonnay and decant the Merlot."

"Fine, then. Also, have a bottle of Grey Goose, dry vermouth, and olives. Be sure the olives have juice. Dr. Thomas likes his martinis dirty." She gave Morgan a few ideas for the vintage of Merlot. "Any bottle should be okay if it's over $40. Dr. Thomas has to do early rounds in the hospital before they leave L.A. He's a renowned heart surgeon. They're scheduled on a one o'clock flight."

The instructions and questions went on for several minutes: Is there parking? Is there a swimming pool? Can they walk to the nearest restaurant? How far is it to the Green Cat Guest House, the venue for the wedding they planned to attend?

"You and your client really should look at my website," Morgan said, trying not to lose her patience. "Morgan Hill Retreat is a bed and breakfast on a five-acre farm, between Poulsbo and Port Gamble. There is no swimming pool or gym. We have plenty of parking, and we're about six miles from the Green Cat Guest House. Please tell them not to use MapQuest. They'll find themselves on the Kingston ferry, but the Bainbridge Island ferry is much closer. Be sure they use the directions on my website."

Morgan and Howard got in the truck to go back to town for the items requested by the travel agent.

"What's *your* favorite Merlot?" Morgan asked the wine merchant.

"I like Apex. It's made in Washington, and it's $35 a bottle."

"I'll take a bottle of Apex, please," she said.

Morgan walked across the street to the state liquor store to get the vodka and vermouth, then drove to the grocery for a jar of olives, thinking, *This is a lot of alcohol for two people for just three nights.* The next day, she ran Dr. Thomas's credit card for accommodations, plus $60 for the Merlot. She marked up everything else by forty percent. She decanted the wine as the merchant recommended, expecting Dr. and Mrs. Thomas to arrive about six-thirty or seven.

At 11:00 p.m., they rang the doorbell. Dr. Thomas had decided that directions on the website were incorrect and printed out Google Maps. From the Kingston ferry dock, Dr. Thomas followed GPS to a neighbor's house. Morgan learned later that they had entered without knocking while the neighbors watched TV in their pajamas.

Dr. and Mrs. Thomas were both about five-foot-two, and Morgan guessed they were fiftyish. He had a pleasant smile; her smile revealed a lack of facial elasticity. Long, unnaturally black hair overwhelmed the woman's too-tight face.

They followed Morgan to the Sunflower Suite where she asked them to complete the check-in form. When they ignored her, she asked, "What time would you like breakfast?"

"We'll have breakfast when we get up, whenever that is. We can eat in our room, can't we?" said Mrs. Thomas, looking down her nose, even though Morgan was more than six inches taller.

"Of course. Call me when you're ready. Here's my cell number." Morgan pointed to the number on her business card. "It's easier than trying to find me."

Before going to bed, Morgan set the breakfast table for the party of five Germans who hadn't returned from their day of sightseeing. She readied the tray for serving breakfast to Dr. Thomas and his too-tight wife from L.A. Morgan left the front door unlocked for the Germans who left their key behind. The doorbell rang at midnight. Mrs. Thomas had locked them out.

The next morning, the phone rang in Morgan's private quarters. "We want our breakfast now and the coffee isn't ready."

"Oh, I'm so sorry. Is the coffee pot in your room out of order?" Morgan smiled, knowing that Mrs. Thomas did not intend to make her own coffee. "The pot in the kitchen is ready to start. I'll be right down." To Howard she said, "We'll go for a walk later. Meanwhile, you're safer hiding up here."

Mrs. Thomas met Morgan in the kitchen by the big coffee pot. Morgan pushed the button.

"Can't we eat here?" She pointed to the table set for the still-sleeping Germans.

"I'm sorry. It's ready for the group upstairs who should be down any minute."

"Is liquor more expensive here? I saw your bill."

"I don't know what the prices are like in L.A. I did mark it up."

"Oh...We'll need fresh wine glasses, a fresh martini glass, and more bottled water."

Morgan assumed she approved of the Apex Merlot; otherwise, Mrs. Thomas would have complained. *She has no idea,* Morgan thought. Morgan turned on the griddle and retrieved stuffed French toast marinating in the fridge, made with the hens' fresh eggs, artisan raisin-pecan bread, her homemade quince jam, and cream cheese.

"Ick! What's that?" Mrs. Thomas stuck her tongue out between her duck-like Botoxed lips. "I don't eat bread." She patted her size-minus-one hips.

"It's stuffed French toast," Morgan said, trying desperately to use her customer service voice. "Your agent didn't indicate any dietary restrictions when I asked." She wanted to remind Mrs. Thomas that she had ignored the registration form.

"Don't you have eggs?" the guest whined.

"I'd be happy to scramble an egg for you." Morgan didn't offer any other alternative.

"Yes," Mrs. Thomas said, fidgeting with the silverware set for the Germans.

Morgan cracked an egg into a bowl.

"Not now! When I'm ready. Why isn't that coffee done?"

"This pot is a little slow, but it makes great coffee," Morgan placed her hand on top of the coffee maker. "I'll bring it to your room as soon as it's ready."

The woman waited with a scowl until she'd had a sip of black coffee.

"Do you want a cup for your husband?" Morgan asked.

"Oh, I guess that's a good idea. He likes cream in his."

As Mrs. Thomas returned to her room, Morgan noticed her jagged, sulfur-colored aura. Wearing the glasses, she often saw the colors, but running the B&B left little time to study their meaning.

Later, when Mrs. Thomas waved from the bedroom door, Morgan set the breakfast table in their suite and served orange juice and fresh strawberries with her homemade yogurt.

"Call me when you're ready for the rest of your breakfast," she said, closing the door behind her. Morgan couldn't help noticing that the aura around Mrs. Thomas looked stagnate and interrupted.

While Morgan served the Germans, Mrs. Thomas waved from her bedroom door again. As soon as she could, Morgan served breakfast in their room. A scrambled egg for her and stuffed French toast lightly dusted with powdered sugar for her husband, both plates garnished with edible yellow nasturtiums and sprigs of lavender. Dr. Thomas seemed delighted with his meal, as Mrs. Thomas helped herself to a bite of his French toast.

"Do you have everything you need?" Morgan asked, standing behind Mrs. Thomas, facing her husband on the other side of the small round table.

He nodded, "Yes, thank you," while his discontented eyes seemed to say, *Never*.

He deals with her every day, Morgan thought.

That afternoon, Mrs. Thomas wandered into the kitchen, making conversation while she waited for her husband to finish his phone conversation on the porch.

"All he does is work. I can't believe he took time to come to Jen's wedding. He did three surgeries on Wednesday." Then she added, "I was an actress in L.A. before I married my husband."

Morgan continued to empty the dishwasher while muttering, "That's nice."

"How long have you been here?" the woman asked.

"This is my second season."

"Where were you before?"

"I worked in marketing all over the world. Before I bought this place, I lived in a condo on Capitol Hill in Seattle." People usually found it interesting that she had moved from an urban condo to this rural setting but Mrs. Thomas had stopped listening. She let out a small gasp.

"You mean you OWN this place?"

"Yes. Yes, I do."

"Who does all the work?"

"I have a cleaning lady once a week. The rest is up to me."

The duckbill mouth gaped with astonishment. Too-tight eyelids stretched over surprised eyes, while the Botoxed forehead remained stationary.

～

Saturday morning, Morgan offered a self-serve breakfast in the dining area for eleven overnight guests.

"This looks wonderful," offered the improved Mrs. Thomas, who couldn't be nicer, now that she knew Morgan owned the inn.

"Thank you. Plates and silverware are on the table. You're welcome to take your breakfast outside or to your room." Four tables on the porch were covered with white tablecloths and decorated with flowers from Morgan's garden.

"Fresh figs and Stilton cheese, what a great idea." Then Mrs. Thomas opened the dish on a warming tray. "Oh good, scrambled eggs. Your hens lay delicious eggs."

Around two o'clock, as Morgan carried the vacuum to the rooms vacated by the Germans, she found Mrs. Thomas in front of the open refrigerator as if watching TV. She wore an expensive-looking white silk blouse with a jacquard weave. Her tiny frame turned to face Morgan. "I just need a little something to tide me over."

I don't serve lunch here, Morgan thought. "How about some of the Stilton cheese and fresh figs left from breakfast?" she said aloud. Mrs. Thomas nibbled half a fig, finished the cheese, and returned to her room leaving the plate on the table without a word to Morgan.

Then Morgan vacuumed, dusted, and rushed to put clean sheets on the beds so that new guests could check in early and dress for the same wedding that Dr. and Mrs. Thomas were attending.

On Sunday morning, while Morgan prepared breakfast, the guests told her that Dr. and Mrs. Thomas lived in Bel Air, with live-in servants and no children, in a huge mansion once owned by Paris Hilton.

"She's an alcoholic and made a fool of herself at the reception last night. When the bartender cut her off, she mixed citronella mosquito repellant in her drink instead of vodka. Apparently she suffered no consequence."

"Would you like more coffee?" Morgan said, holding the pot for the gossip. *That explains the wine and martinis,* she thought.

Mrs. Thomas came out of her room, her petite frame overwhelmed by the cream-colored spa bathrobe Morgan provided for all of her guests. "Do you have any Alka Seltzer?"

Morgan pulled a box from the cupboard and gave it to Mrs. Thomas with a glass of water.

"Don't you have bottled water?"

Actually, I have my own well, Morgan thought, as she retrieved a bottle from the pantry. She realized that this woman struggled to continue her L.A. lifestyle while visiting a bed and breakfast in rural Western Washington. Mrs. Thomas didn't see the magnificently feathered hooded merganser creating a shower of sunlight by slapping his wings on the pond. She missed the great blue heron stalking little green frogs among the cattails. Her window and blinds remained closed to the wispy fuchsia sunrise and lingering scent of lavender. The rock lined path of the labyrinth created no curiosity.

After the other guests left at the designated checkout time, 11:00 a.m., Morgan scooped llama manure in the pasture with the glasses slipping to the end of her nose. Dr. and Mrs. Thomas walked toward the gate at 1:30. Morgan quickly put the rake and scoop out of sight and adjusted the glasses, noticing that the aura around Mrs. Thomas had softened. She seemed more natural and comfortable than when she arrived.

Luna, the cinnamon-and-white llama, walked to the fence, expecting a carrot. When Mrs. Thomas reached toward her long neck, Luna backed away. "They're friendly but not cuddly. They don't like to be touched."

"She's so dirty. Don't you brush them?" said Mrs. Thomas, wrinkling her nose below her stationary brow.

Morgan pointed across the pasture toward Lars, rolling in the dirt, "There's Lars taking a bath, a llama's idea of keeping clean. The dust keeps the flies away." Tillie and Ted Toulouse Goose honked softly at Morgan's feet, as if participating in the conversation.

"Thank you for a wonderful time at your beautiful farm," said Mrs. Thomas with tears in her eyes.

"The food was great, and I never slept better," the surgeon added.

"I've lived in L.A. all my life and never saw a llama or a chicken or a goose. I can't believe you do all of this alone." Mrs. Thomas's long, dyed hair swayed as she wiped a tear.

"The pleasure is mine. I love sharing my farm," said Morgan, trying to conceal her astonishment. "I hope you have a relaxing trip back to L.A."

Once safe from Mrs. Thomas's circle of helplessness, Morgan tried not to judge the woman's choices. She lived in L.A.—Bel Air, no less—with movie stars and billionaires. The rewards of self-sufficiency remained as foreign to her as idleness to Morgan. Mrs. Thomas felt no fire for individualism or spiritual awareness. The financial dependence on her husband far exceeded any feelings of autonomy. Like so many women, she lived a secondary life without a second thought—or any thought at all.

Morgan often watched movies in the guest rooms as she cleaned. One day she found herself mesmerized by a short film, *A Celtic Pilgrimage with John O'Donohue.* With tears and swollen eyelids, she watched it repeatedly. The Irish blood running in her veins recognized the rocky Irish landscape near St. Colman's Well in County Clare, and the lilting cadence of O'Donohue's Gaelic dialect felt like sacred spring water washing over her.

While researching the energetic phenomenon revealed by the glasses, she'd discovered that Celtic Shamans smudged with white sage and sweet grass to clean away negative energy. She placed an online order at Taos Herb Company; however, with so many guests coming and going, the package had waited on a shelf in the pantry.

On the Monday afternoon after Dr. and Mrs. Thomas left the inn, Morgan found the box of smudging supplies. Before stripping beds and doing laundry, she placed a few pale green sage leaves and bits of dry sweet grass in a huge abalone shell she had brought home from India. Using a long butane fireplace lighter, she lit the herbs and gently blew on the embers. Herbaceous, pungent sweetness rose to the kitchen ceiling, swirled around the dining area and into the rafters above the living room. Holding the smoking shell, Morgan slowly walked under the cathedral ceiling, allowing more herbal-smelling smoke to curl through the high beams and the landing above. She entered the Sunflower Suite vacated by Dr. and Mrs. Thomas. Not sure what to do or say, she fanned the sweet herbal smoke around the room, over the bed, and into the bathroom, then put the ash-filled shell on the tile counter in the bathroom. Sitting on the bedroom carpet with her back against the wall, she watched *A Celtic Pilgrimage with John O'Donohue,* again.

A year before, she would have considered the smudging ritual foolishness. Now, however, she noticed that the room began to feel different as the negative forces dissolved and positive energy flowed back into the space.

She knew that Mrs. Thomas had experienced a small vibrational shift while staying in this room, just a flicker of awareness that a gratifying life existed beyond money, social status, and outward appearances. Not only had she never seen a llama, chicken, or goose, Mrs. Doctor Thomas had never met an independent, self-sufficient woman like Morgan Hill.

chapter ten – the birthday club

*There is a candle in your heart, ready to
be kindled. There is a void in your soul,
ready to be filled. You feel it, don't you?*

—Rumi

EARLY IN DECEMBER, A LARGE GROUP called "The Birthday Club" booked on-line. When they arrived, "The Birthday Club" turned out to be Biz and Ruth, as well as Morgan's other friends Shirley, Sue, Deah, and Kara. The women arrived with baskets of food and a carrot cake, Morgan's favorite. She hugged each of them as they came through the door.

"We're giving you a weekend off," Ruth told her. "We brought food, we'll do our own linens, and we insist on paying for our rooms!"

"Wow, I had no idea..." Morgan said with wide eyes.

"Sit down and put your feet up," said Biz. "We're throwing a party here!"

"You guys are wonderful. I didn't even know you all knew each other."

"We didn't." said Biz, "Sue, and I got together and planned it. A little sleuthing got everyone on the same ferry out of Seattle. Ruth organized everything of course."

The women served hors d'oeuvres and set out plates, silverware, and napkins while Morgan watched, amazed and *verklempt*.

"Don't even think about serving us breakfast. I brought cinnamon rolls and Peet's coffee. I'll scramble the eggs if Ruth'll gather 'em," said Biz.

"Of course!" Ruth said from across the room. "I'm not afraid of chickens."

Neighborhood friends arrived with bottles of wine and more food, even Mr. Wakefield and his grandson. Before long, thirty people laughed, ate, and told stories about Morgan. Each friend knew her from a different time and place, a unique stage of her life.

After the neighbors left, the women changed into their pajamas and wrapped in the inn's embroidered bathrobes, like college roommates. They had little in common other than their friendship with Morgan. Deah, the youngest, made a living as a social worker for the Seattle school system. Sue, the oldest, and still a beauty queen, ran a very successful interior design business in Madison Park. She had helped Morgan pick the paint colors and some of the furnishings for the inn. Kara did marketing for Microsoft and Shirley was a retired telecom executive. Each powerful personality enjoyed success in her chosen career and shared a similar vibrational energy, which brought them to Morgan.

At the breakfast table, Shirley suggested a reading.

"Great idea. I brought my tarot cards," said Ruth, pushing back her chair.

"Not that kind of reading," Shirley laughed. "I want Morgan to read an excerpt from her book."

"Yes, read for us," they all agreed.

"I don't know how you managed to take of the farm and the B&B and still have time to write a book, but we'd love to hear you read. Do you mind?" Shirley asked Morgan. "Ruth mentioned you were looking for a publisher."

"I'd be honored if all of you could sit still that long. I'll print a few pages."

Morgan went upstairs to her office and returned with an excerpt from the first chapter. Everyone filled her coffee mug and found a seat on the sofa or the floor while Morgan sat in the leather chair by the fireplace, with Howard at her side.

"Ruth's the only one who's read it." Then looking at Ruth, "I made revisions based on your feedback. See if I did okay."

"I'm sure it's even more wonderful."

Morgan smiled her thanks and began reading.

Finding This Place, Chapter One, page 3:

Early morning air cooled the kitchen while sunrise filtered through the peach tree by the window. "Let's bake this bread before the sun gets too hot," Grandma said as she put on the apron that covered the front of her housedress. Although she'd made bread hundreds of times, she asked, "Can you find the recipe?"

I opened her wooden recipe box, and she waited while I searched for the card, then sounded out, "Milk, sugar, salt, shor-ten-ing, and yeast dis-sol-ved in warm water," thinking I was grown up. We mixed the ingredients in a big green bowl, added flour with our hands, then she dumped the mixture onto the flour-dusted counter. As we kneaded, the soft, sticky mixture became firm and resilient.

Flour lingered on Grandma's hands and forearms. I looked as if I'd gone for a swim in the flour sack. "Look at you!"

She didn't really mind.

"While our dough gets bigger, let's dust you off outside." The weathered, green screen door clapped behind us.

I giggled as she dusted the flour from my eyelashes with the corner of her apron and the breeze brushed a white cloud from my hair. Back inside, she let me wipe the floor around my wooden stool with soapy rags. I probably made a bigger mess that she cleaned up later, but her patience felt like love.

I filled the sink with bubbly warm water and washed my four toy bread pans, then shaped tiny loaves with the dough Grandma had set aside for me. I waited on the floor by the oven.

"Are they done yet?"

"Now are they done?"

At last, Grandma removed one pan at a time, holding the precious golden bread high at arm's length, and placed each loaf on the windowsill. "Look what a wonderful cook you are," she said. "Your little loaves are prettier than the big ones."

Once they cooled, we wrapped my little loaves in aluminum foil and found a basket to hold them. My mother arrived with Mark and our sister, Meredith. I told my mother my plans. "I'm going to make little peanut butter and jelly sandwiches for my dolls' tea party." I don't remember my mother being part of those days on the farm, but I do remember the *two-hour drive home in the back seat of her blue 1952 Pontiac. It had big whitewall tires and a white roof.*

I sat with my brother on a beige leather seat watching telephone poles pass by. Meredith's baby chair hooked over the front seat, and Mom's arm flew sideways to hold her steady whenever we stopped or turned.

On my lap, the former Easter basket lined with a yellow cloth napkin cradled four foil-wrapped loaves of my special bread. After my bath, I readied the dolls' table with my china tea set, placing its pink cups and black saucers just so. Each doll and teddy bear waited on a little wooden chair. When my mother tucked me in, I reminded her, "Tomorrow I'm going to make sandwiches for my dolls."

Finally, at noon the next day, my mother placed the four tiny loaves on the cutting board. Barely able to see over the counter, I stood ready, sure I'd be invited to spread each tiny slice.

As though the big serrated bread knife cut my skin, I watched as she sliced a lengthwise gash in each loaf, reducing my culinary creations to hot dog buns.

"Why the tears?" she asked.

She knew my plans. I said nothing.

"Now stop crying and eat your hot dog. Do you want mustard?"

Wrongly forced into service, those perfect little loaves of golden crusty bread became a metaphor for my life, their destiny no longer my decision. The horizontal gash signified the difference between fantasy and life. My mother could have said, "What a chef you are" or "How pretty they look" or "You must have worked very hard. Let's make hot dogs buns so we can all enjoy your bread." She could have recognized the importance of my spirit, my creativity, my talent perhaps. I could have learned a lesson of intent versus effect. Instead, she ignored me, assigning me to the periphery, as real as my dolls' repast. Any remaining spirit was set aside, like a condiment, waiting.

"Wow," said Sue, wiping tears.

Shirley returned to the room with a box of tissues.

"You *must* get this published," Deah said.

"Morgan, did you ever meet my friend Cher?" said Sue. "I think you were both at my Powerful Women's Summit."

"That was the best Christmas party I ever attended," Morgan said. "Was Cher the one with the straight black hair?" Morgan traced a line from her ear to her chin.

"That's Cher. You *must* call her. She's a publisher, and she'll love this book." Sue took the excerpt from Morgan and wrote Cher's phone number and email address on the back. "Call her. You two will have a great time together!"

After a lunch of leftovers, Deah, Sue, Shirley, and Kara left to catch the ferry. They stripped their beds before going and Ruth started the washing machine.

"Do you have Mary Oliver's book about writing poetry?" Morgan asked Biz.

"Haven't seen it."

"I have a copy in the library I keep for my guests." Morgan returned with two small paperback books. "Here's another one you'll love, *House of Light*. Take them with you if you want."

On Sunday afternoon, after the dishes were done, towels folded, and beds made, Ruth and Biz packed the BMW and put the top down, despite the chilly air. "I can't thank you enough. You planned the best birthday I've ever had."

Before they backed out, Morgan gave each a Christmas gift.

"Open them now. You'll need them for the ride home." Biz opened her package to find a cinnamon and white coverlet. Ruth's contained a hat and scarf Morgan had knitted. "They're made from my llama's fiber."

As Biz turned right out of the driveway, Morgan fed the llamas, chickens, ducks, and geese, then returned to the cozy living room. Next to the Chinese dragon on the registration desk, she found an envelope filled with cash to cover her friends' weekend stay, her only bookings that December. Overwhelmed with gratitude for her friends and this magnificent farm, she walked the labyrinth wrapped in a shawl made of llama fiber with Howard at her heels. Warm tears of gratitude streaked her cold face as snow began to fall.

chapter eleven – two-two-two

Bring into play the almighty power
within you, so that on the stage of life
you can fulfill your high destined role.

—Paramahansa Yogananda

AT 2:22 A.M., ICY WIND WHISTLED as staccato raindrops danced on the skylight. Morgan pulled the comforter to her ears and sent a wisp of gratitude to the laboring furnace. The next morning, wearing layers of shirts, sweaters, and a hooded coat, she walked to the barn to feed the llamas while Howard curled on the warm place she vacated. The llamas had slept in the pasture while snow fell. Following her into the barn, they left oval shapes of steaming grass painted in the accumulated snow.

She spent the day wrapped in the coverlet, reading in her bedroom with Howard snuggled close. She glanced at the clock at 2:22 p.m.

Night after night that cold, lonely January, Morgan woke up at 2:22 a.m. The matching red numerals seemed to tease her.

As she walked through the kitchen, she noticed the digital clock on the microwave read 2:22 p.m.

She wrote a check to Puget Sound Energy for $222.00. She began to think that maybe 222 had significance, like a sign or message. Then, one afternoon, the phone rang at 2:22 p.m.

"Hi Morgan, it's Ruth. How are things on the farm?" As always, they discussed recent events and the lives of their children, then Ruth said, "I'm going to my friend Deanna's *reiki* class. Do you want to go with me?"

"What's reiki?"

"It's all about life force energy. Every culture believes in life force. In India it's called *prana* and in China it's called *chi*. Even Western science recognizes that the energy is real but they can't explain it—yet. The Japanese word, reiki, loosely translates as *spirit of universal life force energy*. The class will teach us to enhance natural healing, like a conduit. Some of us are unaware that we use it every day, but I want to learn to do it on purpose. I thought you might want to join me now that you're opening to new ideas."

Morgan respected Ruth's interest in tarot and such things but had never considered how it all applied to her own life. She tried to maintain an open mind. Now that she'd found the glasses, however, Morgan wanted to know more about the light and colors she could see and the energy she felt.

Ruth went on, "On Saturday, we'll learn the basic theories and procedures of reiki healing and the hand positions. Then on Sunday, she'll teach us reiki symbols and how they're used to enhance the strength and distance of reiki energy.

"I don't want to become an energy healer, but I think the class might be interesting. When is it?"

"Class starts nine o'clock on February twenty-second, at Deanna's studio in Wallingford," Ruth replied.

"February twenty-second, that's two-two-two! That number's been popping up everywhere for the last few weeks."

"Check out Deanna's website. Everything you need to know about the class is on there—SoulIncentives.com." Ruth said. "Sounds like they're telling you something."

Morgan didn't ask who *they* were, she wasn't quite ready to know. Ruth often spoke of *them*.

Deanna's instructions suggested that participants dress comfortably and wear purple if possible, so Morgan wore a purple sweat suit. On the 7:00 a.m. ferry, she stayed in the truck, avoiding bear claws and glazed doughnuts in the ferry's café, then stopped at the PCC health food store in Edmonds. She gathered an apple, a breakfast wrap, and a latte. On the way to the checkout counter, something caught her eye—a pair of purple socks.

She walked into reiki class, unaware that she looked like a gigantic, over-ripe, eggplant.

During class, she watched Ruth and the other students practice the techniques with each other. Wearing the glasses, she felt the glow of Ruth's energy, as if Ruth had been practicing reiki all her life. Some of the others students, awkward and uneasy, drew more energy than they offered. Morgan felt like a three-year-old at the sandbox in preschool, watching but unable to participate herself.

After the workshop, more of aware of energetic phenomenon, she began to understand that energy is all there is. Everything is energy. Trees are energy. Waves on the beach are energy. Human and animal bodies are energy. Energy even filled the dark space between the stars.

Some energy matches and feels good.

Some energy conflicts and feels not-so-good.

Although she'd heard it many times, she also understood that her thoughts were energy too. Knowing this, she began to understand why she usually manifested whatever she imagined.

Energy attracts matching energy.

After the reiki class, she rarely noticed the numbers 2-2-2.

chapter twelve – meeting yuri

The real guru is the one who has killed
the idol you have made of him.

—Rumi

After the birthday weekend, Morgan called Sue's friend.

Cher wanted to see the manuscript.

A few weeks later Cher called. "We want to publish your book.

"That's great! What's the next step?" Morgan tried to sound professional on the phone with Cher, but after hanging up she danced around the kitchen, kicking the air like an eight-year-old who just won her first soccer match.

The manuscript went back and forth with the editor until they arrived at a version that satisfied Cher, then the book stylist designed the interior, and the cover designer used one of Morgan's photos in her design. Once the book went to press, Morgan made plans to attend a bookseller's tradeshow with Cher in Portland, Oregon, in September. For the first time since mid-June, not one guest booked a room for the weekend.

She arranged for the girls next door to take care of the animals. As she packed the truck and said goodbye to Howard, she felt a strange flutter, like butterflies in her belly. With every song on the radio, she felt it. With every tree she passed, she felt it. This trip would be a lot more important than just a tradeshow. She knew changes were in her future and the way she lived her life would transform...yet again.

His cerulean blue eyes caught her attention as his barrel-chested, six-two frame nearly filled the doorway to the hotel ballroom. Morgan quickly broke eye contact. Something about him... those bright eyes glistening between jet black curls and a ginger-colored beard. Morgan's heart raced like a schoolgirl's at her first teen dance.

Stop it, she told herself, *you're probably older than his mother!*

As Morgan occupied herself with unpacking a carton, she felt the thrill of publishing her first book combine with the energetic appeal of the burly, young stranger.

His gentleness reached her ahead of his chiseled form. She knew he would be more than a friend.

Cher squealed, "YOOR-EEY, you're here!" stretching out her arms to give him a hug. "Did you have a nice drive from California?"

"I took my time and enjoyed the coast," he said but Cher wasn't listening. Her sharply cut silky black hair swung into her face as she rummaged in a box on the floor.

"You're scheduled to sign your book at two o'clock tomorrow," she said, looking at the folder she pulled from the box as she tucked her hair behind her ear. "Does that work for you?"

"Sure," he said. "Thanks for the opportunity."

As Cher introduced him to the small group of freshly published authors, Morgan tried to imagine what kind of book this young lumberjack might have written.

"Everyone, this is Yuri Bozek. He wrote a self-help book about intuition." Cher pointed to a yellow and green fractal design on dark-blue background that hung among the book cover posters on the wall behind her. Her assistant, Judy, interrupted with a question, and Cher returned to the business of setting up the show.

"Hi, Yuri, I'm Morgan Hill." He shook her hand with a mitt-like, callused palm and fingers worn beyond their years. She quickly released her grip, then absentmindedly rubbed her hands together, ignoring the electrical charge that pulsed as if she'd touched a light socket. "That's my new book—*Finding This Place*," she said, pointing to the poster-size book cover behind Cher.

"Nice to meet you, Morgan Hill. I like the image on the cover. Is that a wind circle?" he asked in a kind and milky voice adding another layer of contrast.

"Yes. I'm surprised you know what it is."

"I spent a lot of time walking in the desert near Sedona, Arizona," he said. "Did you take the photo?"

"Yes, I'm sort of a photography nut. I shot it in the Mojave Desert."

She didn't mention that she and her friends, Biz and Ruth, were visiting Red Mountain Spa at the time. Often, while Biz and Ruth slept in, Morgan walked among the red rocks and warm sand. Through the lens, her linear view of life widened, allowing more light, more color, and exposing waves of heat rising underfoot, a view beyond her Self.

On their last trip to the spa in St. George, Morgan and Ruth had arranged for a local cowboy to take them via horseback to photograph the petrified dunes and ancient rock carvings along the Santa Clara River.

Biz slept in until her scheduled spa treatments.

Ruth, Morgan, and the old cowboy rode in silence as the rising sun warmed their backs. Beneath his hat, jet-black hair streaked with sparkling silver fell in a thick braid down his back. Old and wise, his milky white and chestnut pinto knew the way without the cowboy's guidance. They leisurely crossed the dessert floor toward red-oxide varnished rocks carved by primitive Anasazi. Dismounting near a high wall adorned with three-thousand-year-old petroglyphs, Morgan captured the art on film while Ruth and the cowboy sat in the shadows listening to prehistoric drumming that Morgan had yet to hear.

"We're just in the way here," Yuri said. "Let's check out the show."

Cher stopped to watch Morgan and Yuri walk among the vendors. *They sort of match,* she thought. Morgan's tall slim body topped with wild copper and silver curls, and conservative tweed blazer, contrasted with heavy socks and Birkenstocks. His red beard, broad shoulders, and burly demeanor contrasted with his silk Hawaiian shirt.

Although invisible to Cher, their indigo auras blended into a bright and powerful luminescence, as if happy to see each other at long last.

Morgan and Yuri wandered the harshly lit Holiday Inn ballroom while wholesalers and publishers set up their respective displays, an unfamiliar world to both of them. "It's almost five. Let's find a glass of wine," Yuri said.

"You're reading my mind!"

They easily found the restaurant near the lobby and sat in a quiet corner, away from the Happy Hour crowd.

"I'd like a glass of the Pinot gris, please."

"And you, sir?"

"Merlot, please."

"Separate checks, please," Morgan said to the waitress, then to Yuri. "I'll be ordering dinner too, so I need to get my purse. I'll be right back." She hurried to her room where she tried to pull a comb through her unruly hair. She put on lipstick, grabbed her purse—and the glasses—and returned to the restaurant just as the server brought the wine.

"Good timing," he said as she sat down.

They made eye contact for the first time since he walked into the ballroom.

Business-like composure still eluded Morgan.

"Tell me about your book," she said as she admired the contrast between his black hair and red beard. Perspiration dampened the back of her neck.

"Like Cher said, it's about intuition," he shrugged, as if anyone could write a book about intuition. "What's yours about?"

After swallowing wine to calm her jitters, Morgan said, "It's a memoir about my journey to find my Self and overcome the restrictions of my patriarchal upbringing." Then, as if returning a tennis serve, "Why did you decide to write about intuition?" she asked, leaning forward, her fingers toying nervously with the base of her wine glass.

"I wrote it to help healing practitioners build an intentional therapeutic environment," he said. "Everyone has intuition but most people dismiss what they feel."

Before Morgan could ask about his credentials for writing a book about intuition, the waitress came by with menus.

"Another round, please," said Yuri, glancing at Morgan. "Assuming you'd like another?"

"Of course," she smiled, still on edge in the powerful energy that surrounded him.

Morgan put on the glasses. Through the lenses, she saw his indigo aura, streaked with liquid gold and shimmering turquoise. She felt a sensation of heat between her eyes and an ache at the back of her neck. Something she didn't understand activated in her body. His blue eyes sparkled, triggering an unfamiliar sense of tenderness.

The server returned with the two glasses of wine, and Morgan quickly ordered her meal. "I'll have the grilled salmon and a side salad with raspberry vinaigrette, ," leaving the glasses in place as she handed over the menu.

"I'll have the pasta with marinara sauce, no cheese, please."

Morgan watched the server return to the kitchen. She felt an odd sense of abandonment, as if the waitress represented familiarity slipping from Morgan's reality.

Meanwhile, Yuri looked at Morgan and calmly, automatically read her vibrational field. He intuitively knew more about her than she knew about herself. His knowledge would unfold slowly.

She stared back through the glasses as butterflies fluttered. Heat rose up her spine. *I'm glad I'm so much older*, Morgan thought. *If I were closer to his age, this sexual undertow would ruin whatever this is.* During the thirty years since her divorce, she had dated a lot of men, and she knew that sex distorted a relationship.

She couldn't fathom her inevitable growth and awakening now that Yuri Bozek had come into her life.

Someday Yuri would help her understand the deep stirring she felt. He knew that sex and intimacy floated on discrete levels of human consciousness.

"I want to hear more about your farm," he said.

"Before I tell you about my farm, can I ask you a question?"

"Sure."

She reached across the table, took his hands, and turned them palms up. "I want to know how the author of a book about intuition could have hands as callused and beat up as these."

A laugh rose from deep in his belly. "Very observant. I run a tree removal company. We do ecological tree work for contractors and homeowners."

"You really are a lumberjack!" she said as the server suddenly appeared with their meals.

"Every summer I hire climbers, and I do the stump grinding myself."

"Stump grinding?"

"I own a remote-controlled piece of equipment that grinds stumps out of the ground. Tree work is hard on my hands—my whole body, actually."

Don't even think about the rest of his body, she thought. To Morgan, stump grinding sounded like a metaphor. *I wonder what he's trying to grind out of his life*. "So your work is seasonal, like my inn keeping business."

"Tree work keeps me occupied from June to September, depending on the snow. I write and find odd jobs during the rest of the year."

"Where did you go to school?" He looked like a lumberjack but sounded more like a professor.

"I earned a Bachelor's Degree at Arizona State, then worked as a biofeedback technician. That work inspired the book. Now I'm outdoors all day in the Sierra Nevada near Lake Tahoe. People weren't meant to be confined in a small room with artificial light." He would tell her the rest of his story another day. "What's your background, Miss Tweed Jacket and Birkenstocks? You must have a story too."

Morgan noticed that he paused ever so briefly before taking a bite of his pasta.

"Touché," she said. "I left a corporate career, sold my condo, bought a five-acre farm complete with llamas, and turned it into a bed and breakfast. While my daughter was growing up, I sold my soul to big corporations, then when she graduated, I kept going because I didn't know that *I* wasn't my *career*." She took a sip of wine, and he waited for her to go on. "Now I'm feeding animals, working in the yard, cooking and cleaning for guests—never worked harder—but I go to bed happy and sleep like a Labrador puppy. One good thing about my former life though—I didn't worry so much about paying bills."

"That's the trade-off."

"I can live with so much less than I thought I needed for all those years," she said.

"The slumping global economy is forcing Americans to that conclusion," said Yuri. "So many are tranquilized with trivia, worried about accumulating more and more possessions, and perpetually overstimulated with aural, visual, and mental noise."

"Yes!" she said with a hand over her mouth full of salad. "If I don't have my silent moments every day, I realize I'm not as... awake."

"The chainsaws and the grinder make a lot of noise, but once I finish a job, and the crew goes home, the silence in my mountain cottage is magnificent. Just..." His dark lashes slowly closed over his bright blue eyes. "...stillness."

As they ate, they listened to Bruce Springsteen's *I'm Working on a Dream* blast through the restaurant.

"Are the llamas difficult to manage?"

"They're a lot easier than horses, and I've learned that llamas know more than I do about my guests," she said.

"Meaning..."

She continued what could have been an embarrassing story.

"For example, a couple got out of their car and walked straight to the fence to see the llamas. Lars, the big male, made snorting noises and balanced his front legs on the fence, making himself twelve feet tall. He'd never done that before."

"What happened?"

"They checked in and later that night—they—had sex in the living room."

"You're kidding."

"Wish I were. Guests occupied every room that night. I came downstairs about 1:00 a.m. to turn off the outside lights and check the doors. They had tossed the sofa pillows and back cushions on the floor and used a kitchen towel to protect the sofa from—well, you know. I threw out the towel. I'm so glad I didn't catch them in the act."

"That story gives new meaning to the phrase 'get a room.'"

"Yes—they *had* a room, a really *nice* room, the best at the inn in fact. At breakfast, they seemed emotionless and remote, as if they hardly knew each other. While they ate breakfast with the other guests, I went to the barn just to get out of there. The llamas were clearly agitated. The guy paid cash when they checked out and gave me a bogus address in Oregon. When I went back to the barn later that afternoon, the llamas had calmed down. I don't think they liked having that guy on the property."

"Did Lars sense you were in any danger?"

"Who knows? Maybe he was protecting his girls; he's the only male in the herd. Or maybe he sensed my uneasiness. I wanted to take a shower after that guy checked in. I couldn't wait until they left, even if they hadn't made a mess in the living room."

"Animals know a lot more than we realize."

"Especially llamas. Maybe because their ancestors were Inca," Morgan laughed. "I could tell animal intuition stories all day long."

The waitress came by and asked if they wanted another glass of wine.

"I think I've had enough," Morgan said. *I might do something stupid if I have another,* she thought.

They paid their tabs and said goodnight with a long hug that seemed natural to Yuri.

To Morgan's psyche, however, Yuri's handsome face and sensual body personified other men she'd known. Habitual sensual feelings swirled in his presence. Even so, she knew Yuri was different, as if born on a planet of his own.

That night she dreamed he came to her. When his calloused hands touched her soft skin, she startled awake, sweaty and aroused. The intensity of that touch kept her awake for the rest of the night. The passion felt odd and confusing.

Morgan and Yuri ate lunch together the next day, and Cher teased Morgan afterward.

"He sure is handsome, Ms. Cougar."

"What do you mean? What's a *cougar*?"

"A cougar is an older woman who has sex with younger men."

"Cher—stop it! It's not like that."

"Oh, it's okay with me. You don't need to lie. I'm just jealous."

"No, *really*. He's very sexy, that's true, and my knees go soft when he looks at me with those eyes..."

"Yeah, those eyes!" said Cher with a twinkle.

"There's... well, I... well... I don't know how to describe it. It's way more than sensual."

"I bet it is," Cher snickered.

"Cher! Stop it! He's probably younger than my daughter."

"Since when does that matter? You can pass for much younger than your age." Although ten years younger, Cher's short plump body made her look older than Morgan.

"Cher, please don't. I like him. We have a lot in common. It's not about sex. Stop with the teasing."

Later that morning, Cher's authors signed books for each other and Morgan took pictures of them with Cher and her booth. Some of the authors clowned around, doing Vanna White impersonations with their books and posters. After lunch, Morgan signed her book for a long line of interested booksellers. Yuri and some of the other authors did the same, then Cher took them all to dinner. Afterward, Yuri drank beer with a mystery writer from L.A. while Morgan joined Cher and Judy for a glass of wine.

"Your boyfriend's really cute," said Judy. "His face looks like that movie star, what's his name! The one with those eyes. He played the scientist in *Kate and Leopold* with Meg Ryan."

"Liev Schreiber," giggled Cher, "with fuller lips."

"Right!" Judy and Cher laughed as their glasses clanked a toast.

"Will you two stop it? PLEASE? He's not my boyfriend. We just met."

"Maybe you just met, but any fool can see the attraction. I love the way he looks at you," said Judy.

"I'd love to have those sexy eyes look at me that way," laughed Cher.

"I'll admit, when I was younger, I would have seduced him… or let him seduce me," Morgan confessed. "This is different. I don't understand it either…. Please, don't make it out to be something it isn't."

The server came by. Cher and Judy ordered a third glass of wine.

"One is enough for me tonight," said Morgan. "I'm going to bed. Goodnight."

In her room, Morgan uploaded the photos from her digital camera and emailed them to Cher. Then she noticed that every image of Yuri included small circles of light, orbs on his shirt or near his head. Morgan checked the lens for dust or water spots, then realized a dirty lens would have caused similar distortion on the other images.

In her dream that night, she and Yuri were young adults. Dressed in odd hand-woven clothing, they kneaded bread dough together. Their arms touched lightly as they pushed the loaves of bread into a wood-fired oven. The intensity of their love completed her, as if until they met, she knew only part of her Self.

She went to breakfast early, planning to read Yuri's book while she ate. When she entered the restaurant, she found Yuri with a copy of her book next to his cup of black coffee.

"Guess we had the same idea," she said.

"Join me," he said, motioning to an extra chair. "To hell with what Cher and the others think."

"Did somebody say something?" Morgan said with wide eyes, mortified.

Yuri knew what others were thinking, but not because anyone had said anything. Like so much in his young life, he just—knew. "Don't worry, this event will be over this afternoon, they'll all go back to where they came from, and we'll never see them again."

She sat across from him, moved by his choice of words… *we'll never see them again….*

She ordered a latte and a Western omelet.

"I hope I'll see *you* again," he said, those eyes melting her heart.

"Me too," thinking how unlikely another meeting would be. "If you're ever in the Northwest, come over to my B&B near Port Gamble. Lars would love to meet you."

"And I would love to meet Lars. I've never met a llama." He smiled that kind, bright smile. She felt comfortable, as if she had known him longer than forever.

Cher walked in, looked around the room, and saw them. Morgan waved. "Cher! Join us."

"Oh, I don't want to intrude," said Cher, assuming they had spent the night together.

Morgan gave Cher a *cut-the-crap* look and pushed out a chair with her foot. Cher sat down. More authors soon joined them, pulling extra chairs from the adjoining table.

"What's on the agenda for today?" asked the mystery writer.

"The remaining authors will sign their books. Some well-known authors have readings scheduled; the list is by the elevators. Since all of you are first-time authors, you should attend as many as possible and introduce yourselves to the wholesalers and store owners; try to schedule readings and book signings in the stores if you can."

After breakfast, Morgan went to her room to brush away latte breath. In the elevator on the way back down, she introduced herself to the owner of Dauntless Books.

"I love your store," she told the owner, Lyn. "I've been going in there for years."

"Glad to hear it. Hey, you signed a book for me yesterday, and I read a lot of it last night. We should schedule a signing sometime soon."

"That would be great," said Morgan, trying to be professional. They exchanged business cards as the doors opened.

"I'll call you," said Lyn.

Morgan thought, *I never dreamed I'd be signing my own book in that store.*

At 4:00 p.m., Cher and Judy started packing up the booth. Yuri, Morgan, and a few others helped carry boxes to her car. "Have a safe drive," Morgan said.

"You too," said Cher. "Yuri, are you driving back to California?"

"No, snow came early in Tahoe this year. I'm planning to camp on the Washington coast, and then spend Christmas with some relatives."

"Well, have fun!" she said, climbing into her Volvo wagon. She waved from the open window as she drove toward I-5.

chapter thirteen — yuri arrives

You can only find truth with logic if you
have already found truth without it.
—Gilbert Keith Chesterton

"Merry Christmas!" Yuri called on Christmas eve.

"Yuri! Merry Christmas. I was just thinking about you," said Morgan. "Are you still in the Northwest?"

He heard the loneliness in her voice. "Yes, I have to wait until the snow melts in Tahoe and it's been snowing a lot at six thousand feet."

"What are your plans?"

"I'm spending this week in Port Townsend ringing in 2010 with my cousin. After that, I'm not sure," he said. "I was hoping to find a project or two before I go back."

"You should come stay at the inn. You're only an hour away."

"Isn't your daughter there with you for Christmas?"

"I wish. She and her husband are in Barbados for the holidays. I'd love to see you. My guests leave early January first to catch a flight back to Michigan. The inn will be empty."

On New Year's Day, while Morgan reset the guest rooms, Yuri rang the doorbell. He'd shaved his beard and his black curls had grown longer, making him look younger, less lumberjack-ish, and even more handsome. *Stop it,* she told herself.

They took their coffee to the porch and sat in rocking chairs, chatting easily about the unusually mild Northwest winter and the antics of her animals.

The sexual undertow lingered.

In her heyday, she had been with sexy men she couldn't have a conversation with and she'd enjoyed long, intellectual conversations with men who had no sex appeal. She would soon learn that Yuri connected with her on an energetic level—far beyond sex or intellect.

"Where would you like me to park my home away from home?" he pointed over his shoulder toward the back of the house.

Morgan walked to the edge of the porch. "You brought your own guest room!" A shiny silver Airstream trailer waited behind his 2002 red Chevy pickup. He'd parked next to Morgan's 1955 red Chevy pickup, fifty years older, with significantly lower miles.

Somewhat relieved that he would be sleeping in his own trailer, Morgan said, "After you meet Lars and the llamas, I'll show you where to park."

"Sounds like a Nordic rock band," he laughed. "Lars and the Llamas."

Yuri and Morgan walked toward the pasture and the curious llamas lined up along the fence as if participating in a beauty pageant. "Llamas are friendly but don't like to be touched. Just let them smell you. If you put your hand out, like you would for a dog, they'll back away." Morgan leaned forward and Luna sniffed her cheek. Then Yuri stepped to the fence. While Lars sniffed his face, Yuri rubbed Lars's long, soft neck.

"Wow. It took weeks and a lot of carrots for me to get that close to him, and he still won't let me rub his neck."

"He knows I mean no harm."

A strong, involuntary sigh released from Morgan's lungs as a weight lifted from her shoulders. She suddenly felt extraordinarily safe with Yuri. Slowly backing away from the fence, Morgan turned toward the trees behind the house. "I'll show you where to park the Airstream."

"Are there fish in there?" Yuri asked as they passed the pond.

"It's stocked with trout. I see them working the surface sometimes in the evening."

Quiet, burbling sounds came from the waterfall on the other side of the pond.

"Where does the water come from?"

"There's a natural spring from underground. That little waterfall never stops. In the winter, rain collects here too and causes the stream to run through the pasture until the rain stops in June." She pointed toward the pasture to the west. "Then the pond goes down, the stream dries up and you can see the path of dry rocks until the rain starts again in November."

"Constantly changing… it's beautiful. Was the labyrinth here when you bought the farm?"

"No, I built it before I opened the inn. I had quite a battle with that rented rototiller! I'd seen labyrinths all over the world but I really didn't know what they were. When I moved here, I thought it would provide a nice ambience for my guests. Turns out, I love it too."

While on a business trip to Paris, Morgan's interest in history and architecture lured her away from the office to the flying buttresses of the six-hundred-year-old Chartres Cathedral. Entering the nave, she found a circular stone pattern covering the cold, stone floor. Automatically stepping into its twisting circuits, she dismissed the sense of belonging and gratitude that threatened to overwhelm her and quickly returned to the familiarity of her hectic corporate life.

A few years later, she discovered a labyrinth in St. George, Utah, while vacationing with her friends, Biz and Ruth. At dawn, as her friends slept, she photographed long shadows cast by the rising sun on the red sand. Again, she rebuffed the powerful tug of the path.

After opening her B&B, Morgan arranged a meeting with the owner of a nearby health spa, hoping to organize a marketing package for potential guests. As she parked the car, she noticed a circular pattern marked by smooth beach rocks. She stepped onto the path covered with long fragrant pine needles. The labyrinth beckoned in a silent, primitive dialect. This time she heard its plea.

She researched labyrinths and discovered that relics and cave walls all over the globe exhibited similar designs long before the Christians adopted the pattern for worship and contemplation. She began construction of a seven-circuit Cretan labyrinth between the pond and the new lavender beds, hoping it would help quench her longing for stillness and reflection.

As with the lavender bed, the rototiller pitched and roared as she removed sod and collected rocks from the overturned soil. She used stakes and baling twine to measure and map out the circuits and placed rocks to indicate the permanent path. Among the rocks, she planted woolly thyme to provide a soft green carpet where bare feet could connect to the earth. By fall, the combined scent of lavender and thyme permeated the air as she walked the circuits. Moving toward the center, the cerebral blare diminished. In the center, she found the calm she needed, and her heart swelled with gratitude.

Beyond a *PRIVATE AREA* sign, they walked through a grove of cedar trees to a clearing. "When I bought the place, I planned to build a little cabin here, where I could get completely away from guests…. It has all the hook-ups, and Wi-Fi so you should be quite comfortable."

"I could build you a cabin in a month or two. I built mine in Tahoe."

"If the economy were better…," She paused. "That is, if bookings were more consistent, and if the real estate market were good… if I knew how long I'd be here…." She laughed. "That's a lot of *ifs*. Really, there's enough for me to take care of all by myself."

They walked to a bricked-in fire pit between the pond and the campsite. From the Adirondack chairs, the snow-covered Olympic Mountains loomed clear and bright. "When my friends come over, we hide from the B&B guests back here…. Do you need me to help you back in?"

"I'm used to doing it alone and the spot is plenty wide. No worries."

"Then I'll leave you to it. Come on in when you get settled."

He backed his trailer into the space, hooked up water, electricity, and septic. Then he found the wheelbarrow and moved a stack of firewood closer to the fire pit about twenty yards from the trailer. *Perfect,* he thought.

Morgan sat at the kitchen table, making a list of projects on a yellow tablet. She'd assigned each a priority, timeline, and cost. When he came in, she gathered her courage. "If you're not going back to work in California until the snow melts... and if you want to... I need help with off-season maintenance... and if you're not working, and... if you want to..."

"That would be great. I packed tools in case I found work."

"I started a plan before you got here, thinking you'd be sleeping in a guest room.... Still, it would be silly for you to eat meals alone out there.... Whether you decide to stay a week or until the snow melts, we need a plan."

"I agree," he said.

"Do you cook?"

"I love to cook and I'm pretty good at it," as usual, understating his ability.

"Great!" she said. "If you'll plan lunch and dinner and do the cooking, I'll pay for all the groceries and clean up. I'll eat anything. After ninety straight days of cooking for guests, I don't care if I cook again 'til spring. Of course, I *will* if guests check in. You don't have to serve them too." She tore the yellow page from her tablet and pushed it across the table. "I made a list of maintenance and repairs. If you're available for three or four hours a day, we should get through the list pretty fast. Just depends on how long you plan to stay."

"Sounds like a deal. I'm writing another book, so having time in the morning works well for me."

"Great, you get free food and a pretty nice camp site, and I get a break from cooking and grocery shopping, and a few maintenance projects taken care of.

Later that day, they drove to Central Market so he would know where to shop. "I have an idea for dinner tonight if you want," he said. "It's called deruny[6]."

"Like I said, I'll eat anything if I don't have to plan and cook. What a luxury."

He prepared his Grandpa Bozek's pancake recipe made with shredded potatoes, onions, and apples, served with yogurt.

"I've never had deruny," said Morgan as they sat down for dinner at seven-thirty. "Smells great."

____

6   **deruny** - *Ukrainian potato pancakes*

"Hope you like it," said Yuri, then paused briefly, respectfully, gratefully, before taking a bite.

"I've noticed that you always stop for just an instant before you eat. You did it at the restaurant in Portland." Morgan said.

"My Grandpa Bozek grew up nearly starving to death as a Russian Jew during a time when both Hitler and Stalin tried to eradicate the entire Jewish population."

She heard a tremor in his voice.

"Every meal reminds me how grateful I am that I don't live like he did." He took another bite. "Where do you want me to start tomorrow?" he said as he swallowed, avoiding any more conversation about the persecution and poverty his Jewish grandfather endured in the Ukraine. Yuri had heard the story many times.

In the winter of 1939, a few months after the Soviet Union and Nazi Germany signed the Milotov-Ribbentrop Pact, the Cossacks rode into his grandfather's village, destroying homes and killing the fleeing Jews. Twelve-year-old Louis Bozek and his parents escaped out the back of their home without shoes or coats as the Cossacks rode their horses through the big front door.

Sharp, frozen cornstalks mutilated their bare feet as they ran through the dark fields. Night after night, week after week, they fled toward the Baltic Sea. Sometimes they found food and shelter in barns along the way. They stole coats and ill-fitting boots from a deserted barn. Hunger drained their energy; still, they kept moving, often without food or clean water for days at a time. They narrowly escaped capture and death on many occasions. Louis's father, Yuri's great-grandfather, was among the thirty million Jews who died on the eastern front, shot as they crossed a pasture too close to an armed anti-Semitic Russian peasant. Louis and his mother hid in a wet muddy ditch and never looked back. They eventually found the support of sympathetic Latvians who helped them gain passage on a ship to Canada.

After his mother died in 1941, Louis took a train to New York. He had lived a long life in just fourteen years. Because of his malnourished childhood, he grew to just five-foot-two and suffered with major health issues all of his life. He married in 1947 and had a son before his twentieth birthday, Yuri's father.

By the age of ten, Yuri had grown taller than his grandfather who died shortly thereafter. Yuri looked a lot like his father, who never acknowledged his Jewish heritage. On a scholarship to Harvard in the 1960s, he studied Russian Literature and married a New York socialite, Yuri's mother, whom he met there.

Respecting Yuri's need to drop the discussion about his grandfather, Morgan said, "Tomorrow after lunch, let's go to the hardware store and get a new kitchen faucet. That one is leaking." She bobbed her head toward the kitchen sink. "And we can get everything we need to organize the garage. I've put it off since I moved in."

chapter fourteen — eagle attack

Meditation is achieved at the point
where mind and spirit converge.
—Edgar N. Jackson

WEARING HER BROWN UGG BOOTS and the red polar fleece bathrobe under her coat, Morgan walked the pasture's frosty grass at daybreak with her red mug of hot coffee. Her hair blew wildly in the wind while Howard zigzagged ahead of her, sniffing everything in his path as if reading the morning newspaper, their usual routine when no guests occupied the inn. She noticed that a huge branch from the Douglas fir had fallen on the fence, breaking two boards.

She opened the waterfowl coop. As Morgan sipped her coffee and Howard watched patiently, the geese waddled toward the pond for their morning bath, followed by the bowling-pin-shaped Indian Runner ducks, standing tall, scuttling in V formation. She followed as far as the labyrinth.

In spite of the cold damp air, she walked the circuits and sat on the bench, listening to the natural spring water tumble over rocks by the pond. Solitude settled her mind, erasing her financial concerns, if only for a few minutes.

While sitting in the labyrinth she thought of her own grandparents. How different their lives were from Yuri's family, during the same time in history.

While Yuri's Jewish grandfather, a boy at the time, fled from the Nazis' toward the Baltic Sea, Morgan's grandparents lived quietly on their dairy farm in Ohio, unaware of the carnage and conflict raging in Europe. Edith filled a wooden box with recipes exchanged among aunts, cousins, and neighbors. The scraps of paper told a story of abundance: homemade bread, dried beef, pickles, cheese, canned peaches, apple butter, and elderberry blossom tea.

At lunch, Morgan told Yuri, "A big branch fell on the fence last night. Let's add treated boards to our list of supplies to buy at Home Depot. I'll keep the llamas in the other pasture until we get it fixed."

"I was thinking," he said, "if I mix some peat into the soil around the gazebo garden and under the dogwood tree, the perennials will be healthier when they come up and you won't need to water as much in summer."

"Great idea. I have enough to do when the place is busy. Let's add garden peat to the list."

They took their time wandering through Home Depot, selecting boards, nails, screws, and the plumbing supplies they needed.

As they drove under the Douglas fir, Yuri shouted, "Look!"

A bald eagle stood in the grass clutching a black Indian Runner duck.

Morgan jumped out of the truck, and ran into the yard, swinging her arms wildly over her head. "Stop! Go away! Get off that duck!"

The eagle remained steadfast staring with disdain until she came within ten feet. As it rose into the wind, the duck dropped to the ground.

"Is it alive?" she wondered aloud as Yuri caught up with her. They stood in the wet grass looking down at the injured bird.

Yuri picked it up, "Its heart is still beating."

Looking into the sky she said, "Can't they find rats or fish or something?" Her voice filled with frustration. "Last summer, the eagle got a rooster and left only a few long red tail feathers."

Yuri gently carried the bird into the house while Morgan found the iodine. They washed it in warm water, treated its puncture wounds, then placed it under a heat lamp in a towel-lined box.

They stood over the duck as it lay motionless, sprawled on its back. "I wonder how deep those wounds are," said Yuri.

"At least the eagle didn't take her back to the nest to be eaten alive." She shivered and folded her arms around herself.

"Didn't you tell me you took a reiki class?"

"Yeah, but… I've never tried to actually do it."

"Now you have the perfect opportunity."

Yuri left to unpack the truck as Morgan focused on the injured duck. She knelt beside the box as she pulled the glasses out of her hair and onto her nose. The duck's long neck bent to one side and appeared broken. It couldn't stand up. She placed her iodine-stained palms just above its distorted body and closed her eyes. An amber glow filled the mudroom. With intent, she mentally traced the counterclockwise symbol she learned in reiki class to focus healing energy into the duck.

"I hope this will help you," she said after a few minutes, then she sanitized the muddy kitchen sink and lathered her hands under warm running water to remove the iodine stains. She thought of the similarities between the Japanese reiki healing symbol and the Celtic spirals tooled on the old trunk in the attic. She had seen similar spirals among the petroglyphs in Utah and the labyrinth as well, as if ancient gods had drawn curative symbols from a universal magic hat.

After stacking the lumber near the broken fence and stowing the other supplies in the garage, Yuri came in the back door. "Morgan, look at this." The black Runner struggled to climb out of the box. "You're more of a Healer than you think you are."

"She's going to hurt herself if she keeps that up." Gently, Morgan carried the duck back to the coop to join her team.

The next morning, as the Runner ducks assumed their usual V formation toward the pond, Morgan had difficulty distinguishing the injured duck—except for her crooked neck.

chapter fifteen – yuri's family

*We can easily forgive a child
who is afraid of the dark; the real tragedy of life,
is when men are afraid of the Light.*
—Plato

A SKILLED CARPENTER, YURI SPENT THE AFTERNOON building shelves in the garage using the table saw and other tools he'd stowed in his truck. Around six, he started a fire and served dinner outdoors as they settled into the Adirondack chairs, sheltered by winter darkness beyond the fire's orange glow.

"Tell me about your childhood," Morgan said. "Where did you grow up? What do your parents do?"

"I grew up in Colorado. My father was a professor of Russian Literature at the University of Colorado in Boulder. Guess that's where I learned to love the mountains. Mom taught English there and wrote children's books. No doubt you read them to your daughter. Mom's books were very popular in the Seventies."

"Do they still live in Colorado?"

"They both died in a plane crash before I turned thirty."

"How terrible! Where?"

"Europe. Dad was searching for a book he thought the Germans stole from a museum in the Ukraine before World War II, and Mom traveled with him. Their bodies were never recovered. My parents, and probably that book, are still frozen at the top of a mountain in Switzerland."

Morgan sat in silence, not knowing what to say.

"I don't think they planned to have children. Mom took a year's sabbatical and started writing children's books, then went back to teaching before my first birthday. She took me to her book signings like a circus attraction. I did the readings before I turned three. What better testimonial than a three-year-old reading his mother's books to groups of intellectuals and their children?"

"I can imagine how cute you were, black ringlets and blue eyes. So you were an only child?"

"Did you say only or lonely?" he laughed, but not with his eyes. "They bought a big house and hired a live-in housekeeper, Mrs. Hanover. She had a daughter, Suzanne, about my age. Mom called her Suzie-Q; I called her Q-Zee. I spent more time with them than my parents."

"What did your parents think about your tree work?"

"While they were still alive, I worked in the biofeedback research lab at Stanford. That's where I got my Ph.D. in psychology."

"You have a Ph.D. in psychology?" She stared at him. "You never mentioned that, Dr. Bozek."

"I also earned a Doctor of Physics. Dad wanted his son to be a professional student. When I got back from Switzerland, I quit my job and stayed in their place while I settled the estate. Then I sold the house, bought the truck and the trailer, and drove around the country for a couple of years. I wrote the book about intuition and two other nonfiction books." Yuri leaned back into his chair and looked into the night sky. "Three years ago, I bought a one-hundred-acre strip of mountainside near Tahoe. I built a little cabin at the top and a huge barn near the bottom. It's like an airplane hangar. I put my tractor, all the equipment, and the Airstream in there when I'm not traveling. When Mom's first book won the Newbery Medal in 1972, Dad bought her a little red BMW convertible. It's parked in there too."

A look of wonder lingered on Morgan's face as she searched his features in the firelight.

"There's a big heated room at one end with humidity control for Dad's antique book collection. Old books were his passion. He collected first editions by Dostoyevsky, Tolstoy, Hugo, and Zhukovsky. There's American literature in there too, including handwritten poems by

Longfellow. When I moved the books, I found a first edition of Henry David Thoreau's *Walden*. It's worth about $35,000 by now. I plan to donate the collection to the University of Colorado, someday."

He got up to stir the fire and add logs. Morgan watched him. His face looked young, and despite the serious conversation, he seemed happy.

"Yuri, I want you to know, I never would have asked you to work in exchange for food and lodging if I'd known about the physics and psychology degrees...it's embarrassing. I thought you needed work this winter. You told Cher you were camping until Christmas. An Airstream wasn't the kind of camping I thought of."

"No reason to be embarrassed. I didn't tell you because I wanted you to see me as a laborer who wrote a book about intuition rather than an author with a bunch of degrees."

"You're still *you* either way. I left an international executive career to do laundry, clean toilets, and make beds. My mother still doesn't get it. Sounds like you tried pretty hard to be who your parents wanted you to be."

"More than you know." He stared at the coals, watching the orange-and-white flames invade the darkness. "Q-Zee and I did things that our parents didn't understand. We both had imaginary friends. When we were really little, Mrs. Hanover set extra places at the dinner table."

"Did you always call her 'Mrs. Hanover?'"

"Mom insisted. She didn't want me to call Mrs. Hanover 'Mommy' like Q-Zee did. I rarely had a meal with my parents even when they were in town, and they traveled a lot. Once, while they were in Europe, Mrs. Hanover caught Q-Zee and me in a dark closet; we were about four, I guess. We filled the darkness with colorful light that Mrs. Hanover couldn't see. She thought we were hiding from her. A few years later, she took us into the mountains for a picnic at a big playground. Q-Zee pushed a little girl on a swing while I coaxed a boy down the slide. *We* could see the children, but Mrs. Hanover couldn't. In fact, that day, Q-Zee and I played with a lot of children that Mrs. Hanover couldn't see."

"Were they spirits of kids that died nearby?"

"Not exactly. I suspect they appeared as children so Q-Zee and I could relate to them."

"Mrs. Hanover was okay with setting the table for imaginary friends. How did she feel about a playground full of invisible kid spirits?"

"She got very upset. When she told my parents, Mom tried to keep me away from Q-Zee, but she didn't want Mrs. Hanover to leave, so Q-Zee and I went to see a child psychologist. I stopped telling the grown-ups what I saw, but I could never get Q-Zee to talk about any of it again. I always thought that someday she'd remember."

"How sad."

"You're not surprised that we saw the spirits?" he said.

"Not really. I'm certain that children see and know all kinds of things that adults 'teach' out of us by the time we go to kindergarten."

"When I was about twelve my parents took me to Russia and the Ukraine. Ironically, Grandpa Bozek was twelve when he left there. We visited the Dnieper River, near Grandpa's birthplace. That's when everything changed."

"Changed?"

"We visited the Monastery Caves in Kiev where people lived and worshiped in underground passages, even before recorded history. The walls were covered with petroglyphs like snapshots of their lives—with drawings of huge draft horses pulling wagons full of timber, plowing the land, and people harvesting crops." He looked at Morgan with a curious squint. Something seemed familiar but he couldn't get in touch with the memory. "As we walked through, I saw the dead Healers."

"Mummies?"

"Spirits. Walking around. The original people living in the caves were advanced, enlightened beings. I could hear them praying, chanting, singing, playing string instruments. By then I knew better than to mention what I saw to Mom and Dad. That's when I met my spirit guide for the first time. His name is Lasalle." He waited for Morgan's reaction.

"I've been reading about angels and spirit guides. Sonja Choquette, Wayne Dyer, Doreen Virtue—many authors write about them. You're the only person I know personally who admits talking to them. How do you know when Lasalle is with you?"

"At first, his omnipresence drove me crazy. I was twelve and arrogant as hell, but then I started to understand that he could help me feel better about myself, even when my parents... well... they were busy with their own lives. Like I said before, I don't think they planned to have children."

"Do you actually see him? Like a human?"

"Not like a human, more like energy in my head. If I need him to appear, he looks like an older guy, nothing unusual. What about you?" he said. "How long have you been talking with your guide?"

Beyond wondering how he knew such things, Morgan admitted, "Just since finding this place. When I moved in, I was still pretty numb from my corporate career."

"Corporate America will do that to you."

"Then I found these glasses." She took off the glasses and looked at them like a treasured friend. "That's when everything changed for me."

"What do the glasses have to do with anything?"

"When I'm wearing the glasses, I see things, hear things, smell things. It all disappears when I take them off."

"Interesting," he said quietly. "Can you see your spirit guide?"

"Right after I found the glasses, a woman appeared like a shadowy hologram in the labyrinth. I felt as if she welcomed me to this land. The yellow wool shawl over her shoulders waved in the breeze and her long, narrow face had deeply weathered skin. Her red hair was like mine only a lot longer." Morgan combed her hair with her fingers. "She had a rose-colored glow around her but I don't think she was a guide. My guides are like a group of genderless consultants who support me. I can't tell if they're men or women. I usually don't see them, not with my eyes. It's difficult to talk to them, and it's even harder to explain. At first, one of them frightened me. Its essence appeared different from the others, like it had another motive for being here, and it didn't have a face."

"What did you do?"

"I asked the being what its name was, "WHO ARE YOU? WHY ARE YOU HERE?" It went away and I never felt that energy again. I have no idea how I knew to do that." Morgan took a deep breath and looked up at the night sky.

"Did the woman in the labyrinth frighten you?" he asked.

"No! That's the really weird part. I felt no fear at all. I could see her face, it was odd but beautiful. In fact, she was quite comforting, like a grandmother or dear aunt might be."

"Is there one spirit who seems more in charge?"

"Well… Sammy, I guess."

"Sammy?"

"It's not that Sammy's in charge really, more like a coordinator. If I need help with a specific thing, either Sammy helps me or assigns the best guide for the job, as if they're all sitting around a big conference table, discussing what's best for me. Sounds crazy, that's why I haven't told anyone about it—until I met you. The glasses made all of this possible."

Although Morgan was unaware of him, Sammy had been her champion on earth since her birth. He had known her higher Self since before she came to the planet, when they discussed her pre-incarnate goals. With Yuri's assistance, she began to understand the extent of Sammy's influence in her life.

"Where did you find the glasses?" Yuri asked.

"They were in an old trunk Mom gave me. It originally belonged to my great-great-great-grandmother," she said.

"How long were the glasses in the trunk?"

"That's hard to say. It sat at the foot of my bed for over twenty years after Mom gave it to me, before I explored the things Grandma left in there. I assume Mom put the glasses in the trunk sometime after Grandma died."

"Are you sure the glasses belonged to your mom's mom? Could they be older than that?"

"Yuri, since I met you, I know that anything is *possible*. The eyeglass case they were in looked sort of Art Deco. I figured they were turn-of-the-century, so they must be the ones Grandma Edith wore in family photos. I suppose someone could have put them in that case later on. Mom refused to talk about them… she encouraged me to find more fashionable glasses."

"So the trunk was passed down to you on the female side of your family. May I see it?"

Chapter Sixteen — The Attic

*When I am silent, I fall into the place
where everything is music.*

—Rumi

Yuri's big shoulders emerge through the light from the landing below. A shaft of hazy blue moonlight cut diagonally from the gable window lighting the trunk like a celebrity on stage.

"Do you see the glow around the trunk?" Yuri asked. "It has its own light."

"The glow seems brighter than before. I've never been up here when it's dark out. Now it's really bright," said Morgan as she put Howard on the floor.

"Family heirlooms become imbued with light, love, and memories. I've seen it in some of my Dad's old books. Even without the glow, it's a beautiful piece. The artistry is flawless. Why did you hide it up here?"

"It decorated the living room for a while." Her fingertips swept over the rounded top of the trunk. "I saw one old guy prop his foot on it to tie his shoes, and a woman balanced her coffee mug on top while she put on her coat. When I caught a little girl climbing inside to hide from her brother, I decided to move it. My friend Biz helped me carry it up here."

As Yuri traced the Celtic designs tooled in the leather, the trunk's luminescent glow shimmered like liquid crystal finger-paints encouraged by his touch. "May I look inside?"

"Of course. You're the only person I know who'll actually see the memories and love it holds."

Howard sat in the shadows, smiling as if waiting for the humans to discover the story he knew.

Yuri raised the heavy lid. "Remarkable," he breathed.

Morgan watched Yuri, aware that he *saw* far more than she had seen, even when she wore the glasses. After a few moments of silence, reverence, she whispered, "Tell me what you see."

He nodded, lifting the quilt, holding it gently in his arms like an infant. "Memories I see are not stored in my brain—nor yours. What we remember is part of collective memory accessed through an inherent connection among all beings."

Morgan nervously adjusted the glasses on her face and waited for him to go on.

"Your great-great-great-grandparents were powerful Healers.

"Mom said Patrick was a thief," Morgan said in a quiet, reverent timbre.

"Not so. During the Irish potato famine they frightened their neighbors and threatened the church by offering their healing powers to a starving community.…"

Yuri and Morgan watched the true story unfold like a telepathic movie.…

Because their healing powers threatened their neighbors, Áine and Patrick Morgan were forced to sail from Ireland on a ship bound for America. They stowed their worldly possessions in the oak and leather trunk. Its contents included the wedding quilt made by the same Christian friends who demanded their departure. One night on the rolling sea somewhere between Ireland and North America, Áine and Patrick carried the quilt onto the deck. They solemnly walked through the cold, salty gale to the stern of the vessel. Patrick grasped one side and Áine gripped the other. The quilt caught the wind like a patchwork spinnaker. "Mother-Father-Universe, bless the friends and family we left behind, they know not what they do."

Wrapped together as one figure in the dark squall, the wind whipping their clothing and tangling Áine's long red hair, they watched the quilt lift and twist as it disappeared into the starless black sky.

As the storm rocked the huge boat, they returned to their tiny berth. Nine months later, Mary Margaret Morgan was born in the village where they settled, Dublin, Ohio. Fearing for the safety of their children, Áine and Patrick kept their mystical powers secret. Their children, Mary Margaret and Patrick Sean, grew up happy, unaware that they inherited their parents' spiritual talents.

In 1870, Áine and Patrick's son and his bride joined a wagon train for the one-hundred-seventy day trip west to homestead in the Pacific Northwest.

After staking claim to a one-hundred-sixty acre plot of land, Patrick found employment with Puget Mill Company and worked his way from whistle punk[7] to bucker[8]. He had an uncanny sense for the lumber business and soon managed the entire logging operation. His wife taught children of all ages in the lumber town's one-room school before giving birth to their daughter Suzanne Margaret.

They saved every cent they could spare then bought-out other homesteaders and accumulated over one thousand acres of heavily wooded land on a hill between Puget Sound and Hood Canal. As the lumber company harvested timber farther and farther from the canal, Patrick's property became more and more valuable. He sold the lumber from the original homestead, but left one massive Douglas fir at the top of Sawdust Hill in honor of the bald eagles that soared overhead.

Yuri and Morgan sat on the quilt, leaning against the trunk.

As Morgan allowed the significance of this vision to assimilate, Howard barked softly from the darkness under the rafters.

"That's not like him. He hardly ever barks, even to go outside," she said to Yuri. Then to the dog, as she walked toward him, "What is it, Howard? What do you want?"

Again, he barked softly and danced on two legs toward the dark eaves. She walked over to him and leaned in under the rafters. "He found something."

"It's a *clàrsach*," said Yuri as she brought the harp into the light.

---

7   **whistle punk** *relayed information between the worksite and the area where logs were dragged for loading.*

8   **bucker** - *someone who cut trees into manageable pieces after they'd been chopped down*

"Yes! An old Irish harp. I've seen pictures on the web, but I've never seen a real one."

Much smaller than harps she'd seen before, it's maker had carved Celtic knots, spirals, hearts, and crosses, similar to the tooling on the trunk, and drilled holes into the thick box to amplify the sound. When Morgan plucked a wire string, it made a clear, clean sound, not what she expected. She sat on the quilt next to Yuri, supported the base of the harp on her crossed legs, and let the top rest on her shoulder.

"Let's play a duet," Yuri suggested as he jumped to his feet.

"Duet? You have a clàrsach?"

"No, I have a balalaika. I got it when my parents took me to Russia."

She looked down at the harp resting in her lap, "I don't know how...."

"Yes, you do," he said as he slid out of sight. "The music lives in your heart. Don't think, just play."

Even though Morgan had no experience playing the harp, or any musical instrument, her inborn talents would soon be exposed.

Yuri knew that finding this harp hiding in the attic held an even deeper meaning; the details would unfold. He hurried to his trailer, retrieved his balalaika and a shell for smudging a scoop of peat. As he came through the living room, he heard brilliant luminous tones floating down from the attic. A soft smile illuminated his face and love filled his heart.

"What's that?" Morgan asked, as he lit the peat in an abalone shell, then fanned the smoke around the attic with the palm of his hand.

"The fragrance carries the memory of the earth and trees and will help us integrate with the music."

When Morgan's fingers plucked the strings, a rich, earthy tune seemed to play itself. Yuri watched her for several minutes, then melted the balalaika's song into her melody. An assembly of emotions floated into the rafters and hovered, as if coming home to the earth, while colorful orbs like liquid glass floated among them.

"It's morning already," Morgan said, hours later, as golden light filtered through the round window. She lowered the harp into the trunk, like returning a child to its mother's loving lap after a long day at play.

chapter seventeen – dreams

And you? When will you begin
that long journey into yourself?
—Rumi

"Hi, Morgan, this is Lyn at Dauntless Books in Port Gamble. I met you at the book show in Portland. I have a favor to ask."

"Sure, what do you need?"

"The author I scheduled for a week from Saturday canceled. Could you do a reading and sign your books for customers? I know there's not a lot of time for publicity, but my regulars love local authors."

"I'd be happy to."

"My authors usually hang out from eleven to four. I'll send out a press release."

"And I'll put the event on my website and my Facebook page, and Twitter," said Morgan.

Locals and tourists came by that Saturday to meet Morgan, while Yuri browsed the bookstore and explored Port Gamble. Morgan read a few pages and signed books off and on all day. Being an inn keeper had hardened her to the strangers who stayed for days and embezzled her energy, but she enjoyed meeting and discussing her memoir with people who demanded so little of her.

Between visitors, Morgan and Lyn chatted like old friends.

"Do you think you'll write another book?" Lyn asked.

"My dream was to do nothing *but* write. Inn keeping and farm chores keep me too busy though. Maybe some day…"

~

"Do you know anything about dreams?" Morgan asked Yuri as they sat by the fire.

"Usually dreams are personal, but some common symbolism applies to most people. Did you have a good one?"

As she recounted the dream, her voice became gentle and deliberate. "I walked in a cave with a soft breeze that smelled of mud, wild flowers, and baking bread. The dim tunnel twisted back and forth, higher, lower, wider, and narrower with warm packed earth beneath my bare feet. My fingertips traced pointed quartz crystals overhead and followed cold, smooth walls leading to a wide wooden door with symmetrical chevrons of light glowing between huge rough boards. I stepped out of the darkness into a brightly lit chamber." Morgan inhaled the damp night air. "Being in a dark tunnel and not being afraid is a big deal for me. I'm usually terrified of dark, closed-in places," she said, as if returning from a faraway place.

"So you walked through your fear…," he said.

"A glowing button beckoned me to touch it and the heavy door silently closed behind me. I felt as if an elevator lifted me up. Then the door slid aside revealing a glowing garden with tomatoes, corn, peas, and beans. Low morning light saturated everything. The air seemed thin and filled with color and the aroma of dark purple lavender, peach blossoms, and hydrangea of all colors. The fragrance made me dizzy. Long-horned cattle and *Jacob*[9] sheep grazed in tall green grass. I sat on a warm rock bench in the center of the pasture with a blanket of violets under my bare feet…."

"Did you meet any people there?" Yuri asked quietly, so as not to disturb the air around her dream.

---

9   **Jacob** *sheep were first imported to Canada and the United States as zoo animals due to their exotic appearance. They have a spotted or piebald fleece which is genetically white with black spotting. They are small sheep, both males and females can have two, four, or even more horns. The wool is sought-after by hand spinners.*

"No," she said, matching his stillness. "The whole garden, everything, existed just for me. I felt so safe, and I sensed this powerful, overwhelming love. Like I'd melt. Not love for a person or an object, just a deep understanding that love is everywhere... then, I woke up.... What does it mean?"

"I've had a similar dream all my life," he said pensively. "The tunnel, the fragrance, the garden. I'm running in a warm cave and I smell bread baking. At first, there's lots of light, music, and laughter. Then hollow silence and the light is gone, but the feeling of love remains strong."

Morgan nudged the coals with a stick and added a log. Sparks filled the air around her as she slid back into her chair and tightened her purple jacket against the damp night air. Their matching dreams seemed feasible and for some reason, not the least bit surprising.

"Have you always been afraid of the dark and closed-in places?" he asked.

"For as long as I can remember. Even when I was a baby. Mom says she left the bedroom door open and a light on so I'd fall asleep. Maybe someday I'll figure it out; tonight, I'm too tired."

chapter eighteen – meditation

One day you finally knew what you
had to do, and began, though the voices
around you kept shouting their bad
advice—though the whole house began
to tremble and you felt the old tug
at your ankles...

—Mary Oliver, The Journey

"The fire smells different tonight," Morgan said.

"I added a scoop of peat."

"You mean the peat we bought for the garden?" she asked. "Is that what you used to smudge the attic the other night?"

He nodded. "The fragrance is comforting. I smudge the trailer with it when I'm having trouble clearing my mind to meditate or write."

Morgan leaned forward out of her chair, breathing in the aroma and allowing the heat of the fire to warm her face and hands. A faint memory lingered just beyond her reach. "Do you listen to music or tapes when you meditate?" she asked.

"Sometimes… it depends on my focus," he said, staring into the yellow flames. "Sometimes I do visualizations. Want to try one together?"

"Sure."

They leaned back into their chairs.

"Relax, close your eyes, and breathe…. Imagine you're an eagle…. Your orange talons are clutching the top branch of the fir tree…. Breathe…. Spread your wings…. Lift effortlessly into the wind…. Let the current take you higher and higher, above the farm…. See the snow-covered Olympic Mountains and Hood Canal reflecting the clouds. As you float higher, you see Seattle's skyline, the Cascades…effortlessly higher and higher, until you see the Palouse of Eastern Washington, the Columbia River as it flows from Canada to the rolling blue waves and white caps of the Pacific Ocean…. You float higher… and higher…. You see South America, the curve of the planet…. The earth below your huge wings becomes a blue ball, in a sea of darkness, beyond the yellow sun…. Your wings dissolve into air and light… floating higher… higher…. Calmly… open your bill to drink the sun's liquid heat, warming your heart…. Your feathers become the light and your body becomes pure energy as you absorb the sun's yellow heat and drift effortlessly between the sun and the blue planet we call Earth….

"Slowly… reluctantly… you begin your descent… closer to Earth's gravitational pull, closer and closer…. You see the Amazon River and the Great Wall of China… floating… ever closer to the blue ball and its atmosphere…. You see strips of green land and emerald water between the snowy Northwest mountain ranges…. Floating… ever closer… and closer…. You see the lighthouse at Point No Point, Port Gamble's Teekalet Bluff reflecting morning light, and the deep, blue Hood Canal…. Floating back to the Douglas fir that has been your home for centuries… Your golden talons clutch the top branch high above the farm…Your wings fold and slowly you float to the pasture into your human form once again…. To complete the journey, you rub your palms and wash your face with their warmth…."

Yuri and Morgan bathed their faces with heat and light, each filled with gratitude for this night, each other, and the mystical bond that united them beyond space and time.

After a long shared silence, Yuri asked, "How do you feel?"

"Tranquil, calm, filled with… joy. I had no idea meditation like that was possible. It's like I really was floating above the planet, close to the sun. I felt something more… we each became both condor and eagle, melting into the dichotomy, concurrently, like a musical chorus…"

"Wonderful! Someday you'll understand your talents."

She looked at him curiously. "Does it mean anything? Where did I get the condor?"

"In shamanic tradition, the eagle represents the analytical mind while the condor represents the heart. In reality, both birds can fly as high as ten thousand feet above the earth, giving them a unique perspective. I'm writing a book about the historic dichotomy of heart and mind in North American culture. As humans, we need both to navigate the planet. In North America, however, heart energy is often diminished in favor of the mind's analytical powers. It's remarkable that your awareness captured the essence of both birds."

She shook her head and ran her hands through her thick, wiry hair. "What's even more surprising is that I did it without the glasses."

The glasses waited on her nightstand.

chapter nineteen — light show

Once you get hold of selflessness,
You'll be dragged from your ego
and freed from many traps.
Come, return to the root of the root
of your Self.

—Rumi

AFTER A LONG CONVERSATION BY THE FIRE ONE NIGHT, Yuri walked with Morgan to the back door. "Good night," he said and hugged her.

Then Yuri found his balalaika and returned to his chair by the fire. Playing reminded him of his good fortune. He lived an introverted life, writing about abstract thoughts and experiences he would someday reveal to the world. Sharing his views with Morgan, while helping her to understand her own inner essence, provided him with a feeling of freedom and light. As he played, faint memories swirled—string instruments and an agrarian life where dark narrow hallways were natural and cheerful. The tunnel dream they both experienced strengthened his suspicion that he and Morgan had spent at least one past-life together.

The next evening after dinner, Yuri drove to the store for groceries while Morgan cleaned up the kitchen and started a fire in the fire pit. Yuri found her there after putting the groceries away. "Are you crying? What's going on?"

"It's difficult to talk about." She cleared her throat and slid further down into the chair with Howard draped over her knee.

"Even with me?"

"Especially with you."

As he leaned over to add another log, she saw his beautiful aura reflecting streaks of firelight.

He realized they would finally have the inevitable conversation.

"I have this...these...feelings, like a combination of pleasure and pain or an electrical current deep in my...I don't know how to...."

"Like an orgasm?" he said gently, though matter-of-factly. "Don't be embarrassed, I feel it too."

"You do?" she said sitting up straight, finally looking up at him.

"Why is this so difficult for you to talk about?"

She rolled her eyes and slumped back into her chair. "Years of practice. It's about being a good girl, I guess."

"Tell me what you feel." He poked the coals with a long sturdy stick.

"Well, last night when we hugged good night, I felt this—the only word I have is *current*—this current, down there. It came from you, not me."

"First, you need to understand it didn't come *from* me. You and I have a unique situation. We've done meditations and practiced energy work since I arrived. Together, we played the music of our ancestors from universal memory. All these things bond our energy. We trust each other. As a result, we amplify each other. One plus one equals three when we connect. Last night, did the feeling have light or color associated with it?"

"Yes! It glowed bright orange. The feelings and the light frightened me...so I said good night and ran up to my room. Then I cried myself to sleep feeling confused...and...ashamed."

"Your feelings are not shameful. We should talk about this. It's wonderful that you felt the energy and even better that you saw the light. That means you're awakening to the world around you—the life you've denied."

"Are you sure I'm not turning into that cougar Cher thought I was in Portland?"

"Quite sure," he laughed. "Have you ever heard of energy organs or energy centers?"

"You mean chakras?"

"That's what Hindus call them. Unfortunately, that term has been reduced to jargon in some circles. These centers are real and just as important as your heart or lungs—and critical to the existence of all living things."

Something deep in her memory began to pulse. An image of her great-grandmother sitting on a stump floated in her mind. Morgan put her hand on her forehead, as if to retrieve the memory of Great-Grandma Mary Anna's words:

"The body has non-physical centers, as vital to well-being as the heart, eyes, and lungs. Just as your heart knows to beat, it also knows to love. The centers will help you sense your world. They connect your physical body to non-physical parts of your Self. This is true for all humans. Someday, because of your special ability, you will discover how your intent relates to these centers and you will help others understand…."

"Someday you will meet a wise young man who will lead you on the journey of our ancestors. Until then, know that I will always be nearby when you need me."

"Yes, I've heard of the colors and energy centers. I never figured out what they had to do with me or how I feel about anything, especially sex. I've read that there are specific colors associated with each chakra, right?"

"Authors write about the colors they see. My view is that everyone sees his or her own colors. Whatever you see is correct. If you think a certain chakra will be blue for example, then it will be blue. It's all about intent." He leaned forward out of his chair. "Will you try an experiment with me?"

With some hesitation, she nodded.

"Stand up and face me."

She stepped to a comfortable distance.

"Now, remember when we held that ball of light in our hands?"

"Sure, it was incredible," she said.

"Let's take it further. Let your eyes soft-focus. See me from the back of your head instead of with your eyes. Just follow your breath."

He waited for her to relax into his instructions.

"Now, I'm going to let my heart energy mingle with your heart energy. It always happens when we're together except this time you're going to see it and feel it—consciously. Breathe in to the count of five; remember how we did that? In...out...Let's do that for a minute or two. Keep your eyes open and out of focus. Let your mind go as empty as you can. Remember, if you think too much, the light will vaporize."

In the darkness by the fire, a glow materialized between them—heart-to-heart. Morgan saw the glow as slightly green. To Yuri it appeared more yellow. Telepathically, he asked, *Can you see the light? Do you feel the energy?*

She nodded.

"Now, we'll connect the vortex at the top of the head," he said softly as light began to glow above them.

"Allow awareness of your forehead or third eye. Let it be any color that feels right to you. There are no rules; it's as personal as a dream," Yuri said in his deep, buttery voice. "Now the throat. Can you tell me what you feel without making it vanish?"

She cleared her throat. "It makes me want to cough, like when Mom tells me my hair looks awful, or when I try to have a discussion about something she doesn't want to talk about."

"That makes perfect sense. Your mother interrupts from a visceral level. Most people aren't aware of it, even though it's common. The energy vortex near the throat works with expression and communication. When you have trouble discussing something, it gets caught in your throat, you feel a tickle."

Morgan cleared her throat again.

"Just relax. Empty your mind. Let's go back to the heart again. Make its light any color you want... Now, let's move down to the solar plexus. Do you feel the energy?"

"It's lovely."

"Now go further down into your private area. Is this what you felt last night?" he asked softly.

"That's it!" Her voice felt loud in the darkness. The light and sensual feelings vanished. "It's so intense I can't, I can't... not with you."

He laughed in spite of the serious moment. "Morgan, this sensation is as natural and wonderful as any you could have as a human. Why deny it?"

"Because you're... I'm... because we're not...." she took a deep breath. "Because we're not lovers," she said, looking at her boots. "That's not how I think of you."

"Do you understand how we amplify energy when we're together?"

"I think I know what you mean, yes," she said, still studying her Uggs.

"So why wouldn't the reproductive area be stimulated too?"

"Well… that makes sense."

"If I were some hot guy who just wanted to get in your pants, I'd focus on nothing but the second chakra."

"Oh my goodness! What a thought!"

Their laughter pealed through the darkness, reducing Morgan's uneasiness.

"Imagine this lovely sensual feeling without boundaries. No past lovers, or old boyfriends, or making babies—just a wonderful gift of light and love, like the heart light is…. Look at me, not your boots…. Now—soft-focus. Go back to breathing to the count of five. In…. Out…. That's it, just breathe…. Let your heart energy and light meet mine again."

Yuri focused on heart energy to comfort Morgan. He knew she felt safe there. "Breathe…. Good…. Now the solar plexus... slowly... good…. Keep breathing. Now, skip to the base chakra. Some see red or magenta light around this center but like before, you can make it any color you want. This is where we connect to the earth. Good…. Just breathe and let your eyes stay out of focus. Great. Now, if we connect all the centers, the light and connectedness will amplify… just breathe into it. Start at the crown, connect all the way to the base…. Gently," he added in a whisper.

Yuri reached forward and took her hands as a rainbow of colored light arched between them and a soft white orb formed above their heads.

Howard watched as the beautiful light show materialized. His black eyes reflected the glow, his head curiously twisted from side to side, and he panted, as if smiling with joy at their performance. Colorful light bathed the fir and cedar, and the pond reflected the radiance. Then as Morgan's mind returned to thought, the light faded, then vanished.

"This is wonderful. REALLY WONDERFUL. Can you make this happen with anyone?" she asked. *Am I special?* she thought as her ego returned. "Sorry. Never mind. Forget I said that. I know better.... Now is all there is—right now. Now is enough."

She sat down, feeling energized and exhausted at the same time. Howard jumped into her lap. They sat, listening to the tree frogs' frenzied chorus. The crackle of the fire grew louder as they watched tongues of orange flame lick the maple logs.

chapter twenty – light visitors

*One of the deepest longings of the
human soul is the longing to be seen.*
—John O'Donohue

"I saw them before I went to sleep... I think," Morgan told Yuri over lunch one Sunday after guests checked out. "Five beams of light huddled in the corner of my bedroom. Howard sat on the foot of the bed and twisted his neck back and forth. He must have seen them too. They spoke to me, not like people... not with voices. How can I describe all this? It wasn't a dream—I was awake."

"You're doing fine. I think I know what you mean—pillars of light in the corner...."

"Yes, well, they told me not to be afraid, and then I felt love like I've never felt love in my life. L-O-V-E doesn't cover it—like my insides would melt. It felt one hundred times stronger than the tunnel dream. The amazing feeling lasted only a few seconds," she put her arms around herself as if clinging to the sensation, "without any suspicion or hesitation, I absorbed and cherished the feeling of being loved."

"Now do you feel worthy of love?"

"I wish I could just snap beyond past feelings, but the light visitors gave me a touchstone. Now I know how love feels." She took a deep breath and shuddered as her lungs expanded and contracted. "Do you think they were my spirit guides?"

"What do you think?"

"I knew you'd say that."

"Well?" he said.

"What they are is irrelevant. They came to help me feel—really feel—love. Thanks to you, I'm learning to get out of my own way so they can help me."

"Progress," he said. "This is great." He stood and walked around the counter to the stove. "You want more eggs or another piece of toast?"

"I'm full. Great meal as usual! Thanks."

"After I finish these eggs, let's go for a walk."

~

Morgan worked in the office/living room in her private quarters while harp music played softly on her MP3. Usually, when guests occupied the Sunflower Suite and the weather was too wet for a fire, Yuri went to his trailer to write after dinner. This night, however, he stretched out on Morgan's bed and read a book from her B&B library while she reviewed reservation reports. Bookings were up over the previous two years; however, she feared the off-season slump would be too deep.

With the glasses on her nose, she developed marketing scenarios that would boost bookings and lower expenses. She logged into the inn's website and added, "*Whole-House Bookings. Rent four bedrooms and the kitchen for a low group rate. Three-night stay required. No breakfast included.*" While fine-tuning her advertisement, she began to feel disoriented and dizzy.

"Yuri? Can you come in here? I feel sort-a weird."

Yuri put down the book and joined her.

"I'm woozy, my heart is pounding, my palms are clammy. I feel like I might vomit." She rubbed her hands on her jeans and sniffed the air. "Do you smell smoke?"

"Do you have any idea what it is?" Although he knew immediately, he wanted Morgan to discover for herself.

Morgan looked up at him. His calm face suggested the house was not on fire and a heart attack was unlikely.

"Why is it cold? The furnace is blowing warm air but this area is cold." She pulled her arm through the space near her chair.

"Before I tell you what I see, I want to know what you feel. Don't think. Feel."

"If you weren't here, I'd go get a glass of wine, put on a movie, and knit. I'd probably ignore that I felt anything at all."

"Then I'm glad I'm here. You don't want to miss this. Try again. What do you feel?"

"I don't know."

More sternly than ever before, he said, "Don't say you don't know. You do know." Then his harsh tone turned softer, more nurturing. "Has anyone close to you died recently?"

"You don't think it's a ghost? Oh, I don't think I'm ready to go there."

"Sure you are," he said aloud, while telepathically telling her, *You're safe, I'm here to help you.*

"My father died recently," she said.

"Did he have wavy blond hair, a thick waist, and smoke Prince Albert tobacco in a walnut pipe?"

"Yes," she said, her voice shallow, barely audible.

"Your father is here with his guide."

She shook her head, not wanting to believe that Yuri could actually see the spirit of her dead father. "He's here?"

Yuri nodded.

"With a guide?"

He nodded again, giving her time to absorb the experience. "At this stage, his guide is acting as a mentor helping him adjust to being back in nonphysical form," he said.

She closed her eyes, tight, and put her hands over her ears. "He's saying something but I can't understand."

"He wants you to know he's sorry."

"Sorry? It's a little late for sorry. He had sixty years to...."

She felt like emotional chowder: Sad. Frightened. Overwhelmed. Her anger flared like fire set to dry timber.

"He says he didn't know who you were."

"Of course he didn't know who I was. He never *cared* who I was." A childhood of hurt and anger came rushing back. "He knew I was his daughter—didn't make much difference when he was alive." Morgan struggled not to take out her anger on Yuri.

"He just keeps saying he didn't know, and he's sorry. What do you think he means?"

Morgan took a deep, shuddering breath while big tears rolled freely down her cheeks. She touched Yuri's hand on her shoulder as if her fingertips could absorb additional strength.

"I'm trying to step back from feeling like a little girl. Some of the things he did were so ghastly, like taking my brother and me into his office to see mutilated patients. He thought he was teaching us safety..."

With Yuri's hands imbuing his extraordinary energy, she reached dark abandoned places in her heart. "I'm starting to understand how difficult parenting was for both of my parents. Doc had no idea how to behave. His mother was an orphan and only sixteen when Doc was born. When he was nine or ten his little brother died of rheumatic fever. Grandma Hill must have gone cold inside. I never thought about how young and miserable she was during the Depression when Doc was growing up." Morgan put her hand on her chest. "I can feel his loneliness…. He got good grades and he sang and played the cello, but now I see the responsibility of his music. He played for his mother, not for his own pleasure." She stared blankly into the space between them. "He didn't know how to love us.... Besides that, I was an independent little thing from the beginning. How could he know me? Even though I tried, I never behaved the way *he thought* little girls should behave. When I got older, I struggled to grow beyond his *shoulds*." Morgan felt her father's sadness like a cold steel blade deep in her heart. With Yuri's help, her anger and resentment diminished as the air around her grew warm again.

"His mentor, Charles, is saying it's time to go, your father is growing weary. This is difficult work for a newly passed spirit," said Yuri.

"It's difficult work for me too." Still sitting in her desk chair, Morgan put her face in her hands, bent to her knees, and wept while Yuri rubbed her back. Her father's death had caused no tears; his life, however, generated sadness from deep inside. Finally, she sat up. "Intellectually, I'm beginning to understand that he came to the planet for some purpose, but the feeling of rejection doesn't easily melt away."

"Are you still cold and nauseated?" asked Yuri.

"No. I'm fine, except for this ache in my heart." She put her hands on her chest again. "Even now, he didn't say he loved me. He said he didn't know me, like it's an excuse for not loving me." Then she sobbed. Yuri continued to rub her back until the sobs became shudders. Then, quietly, without further conversation, he left her to process her pain.

chapter twenty-one —
all things spiritual

I didn't come here of my own accord,
and I can't leave that way.
Whoever brought me here
will have to take me home.

—Rumi

WITH THE GLASSES AND YURI'S SUPPORT, Morgan became more comfortable with all things spiritual.

One evening in February, Yuri and Morgan lingered by the fire pit after dinner. Yuri said, "Do you realize our guides are here with us now?"

"I think so. Seeing and talking with them seems so strange. I wish I had proof that I'm not going crazy."

"I still have doubts sometimes too. Our world doesn't accept the possibility of multiple layers of life. If you want proof, ask."

"Okay." Morgan stood and made a ceremony of her request. "Please, please, please," she said with her arms stretched into the night air as she turned in a circle. "Prove that I'm not going crazy. Prove that you're real." She sat down. "There, I asked. Do you suppose we'll know anything by morning?"

"Maybe you could be a little less cheeky."

"I know. I'm sorry. Just asking for proof feels uncomfortable and disrespectful…. I'm going to bed. Can we finish the shelves in the garage tomorrow?"

"You can't muscle your way through all this. You'll find your way. Stop trying so hard."

She started toward the house, then turned to say, "At first, the glasses seemed so magical, but the more I learn, the more skeptical I become."

"We'll see what happens. Goodnight." Yuri retrieved his balalaika from the trailer and played by the glowing embers. With the music wafting through the cedar trees, he talked to the spirit of his grandfather, who always lingered near him.

Thanks for guiding me here, Yuri said telepathically.

As always, it is my pleasure to guide you, his grandfather replied.

There's so much to learn. I love watching Morgan's enlightenment develop. We amplify each other's energy. She's still learning what that means. I'm grateful that I can help her and I feel my energy changing as well. I'm capable of even more now that I know her, even if she's unaware that she helps me, Yuri told his grandfather.

I very much enjoy watching your development, and I grow as well. There is always more to learn, no matter the level. My hope is that, through your writing, you can help the world just as you are helping Morgan.

Happy, sweet music rose from the triangular balalaika in Yuri's huge, weathered hands. As with musical meditation, his body relaxed and his energy centered. Beautiful songs lifted into the night, created with just three strings.

Yuri returned to his trailer, hung the balalaika in its place, and opened his laptop. His background in physics and psychology gave him credentials, while Lasalle, his spirit guide, gave clarity and added deeper meaning to the book he worked on.

Your writings will help the planet embrace peace. As you combine your spiritual knowledge with your understanding of physics and human psychology, you can help the world find a balance between heart and mind. In the future, esoteric types of healing will complement drugs and surgery. Egoic thought will give way to caring energy that promotes cooperation among humans. Your writing will lead humanity to rediscover harmonic unity.

Yuri began writing, feeling grateful for the knowledge and inspired by the massive responsibility.

chapter twenty-two —
the letter

*To be born is to be chosen. No one is
here by accident. Each one of us was
sent here for a special destiny.*

—John O'Donohue

EVERY MORNING FOR MOST OF HER ADULT LIFE, Ruth sat in meditation. Her spirit mentor, Alex, appeared during this quiet time, inviting calm into her space, helping her connect with universal love, and providing answers to her questions. One morning, Morgan's guide, Sammy, also appeared in Ruth's meditation.

Good morning, Ruth.

Good morning, Sammy. I've been expecting you. Alex told me you would visit but I didn't know it would be today.

I have a request from your friend Morgan. As her guide, I'm helping to dispel her doubts and fears about her intuitive gifts. Will you be so kind as to help her before your return?

Of course.

Ruth walked to her desk and, using her monogrammed stationery, began to write.

Dearest Morgan & Yuri,

During rainy weeks in February, Morgan and Yuri cleaned the barn, fixed a leak under the sink in the Sunflower Suite, and finished building shelves and organizing the garage. Morgan forgot about her request to the Universe.

Then one day the weather cleared. Rather than building a fire, Yuri put a blanket on the grass near the gazebo garden.

Normally frightened when alone in the dark, Morgan had never spent time stargazing at the big night sky above her farm. However, she felt safe with Yuri as the Milky Way swept over them. The Big Dipper looked close enough to touch. Morgan thought about the distance between the stars, planets, and the galaxies beyond what they could see. The word *infinity* became tangible as she stared into the limitless night sky.

She felt a familiar sound, like an electrical current just beyond her touch. "Yuri, are Sammy and Lasalle watching the stars with us?"

"I wondered if you could feel them." Yuri had seen the holograms of three spirits and felt their intensity long before Morgan noticed. He waited for her to feel them too.

"I can, like a tingle.... Yuri, do you see the woman talking to Sammy?" Morgan didn't see human figures; however, a familiar woman's spirit appeared like a mist near Sammy. "Do you know her?"

"I see her but I don't know who she is."

Cold damp air wafted under the blanket as Morgan suddenly stood up. "Yuri, that's my friend Ruth! I don't understand. Ruth is here, talking with Sammy. She can't be a spirit, she isn't dead. I don't understand."

Ruth spoke.

Hello, Yuri, I'm happy to meet you at last. And Morgan, I'm sorry to frighten you. Sammy and I are here tonight to help you understand. I left my human body after a car accident today. Before getting into the car, I put an envelope on my kitchen counter for the two of you to read after the funeral. I wrote your name on the front of it, Morgan, so there would be no doubt it's for you.

"No! NO!" Morgan ran through the dark to the house as Yuri followed. She dialed with trembling hands. "Hi, Biz, how are you?" she said, trying to keep her voice calm, with little success.

"Morgan, I'm so glad you called. Something terrible has happened. Ruth's been in an accident. I just talked to my brother-in-law, Tom. She's at the Overlake emergency room."

"What happened?"

"Her Jeep was in the shop so she used my convertible to run errands. Some daytime drunk ran a red light and hit her broadside."

"Where are Sarah and Tom Jr.?"

"Sarah is on her way to the hospital. I was just leaving. Tom's calling Tom Jr. in Santa Fe as we speak."

"I'll take the ferry tomorrow. There must be something I can do to help," Morgan said, without breathing, uncomfortable with her deception.

"That'll be great. When she wakes up, she'll be glad to see you...the other line is beeping. I'll call you later."

Morgan looked at Yuri as she hung up the phone. "There's been an accident."

"Ruth?"

Tears covered Morgan's face. "They don't know if she'll survive... I guess... we know... don't we?"

An hour later, Biz called from the hospital to confirm Ruth's passing.

"I'll be there in the morning," Morgan said. After she hung up, Morgan couldn't remember what they had said to each other.

As a human on earth, Ruth knew she was a soul in physical form, rather than a physical body with a soul. She remembered that much. She didn't remember, however, that among her pre-incarnate intentions were two goals: One, help Biz open to the concept of enlightenment; and, two, provide Morgan with proof that multiple layers of existence were genuine. Before she incarnated, she made an agreement with her spirit-friend, Alex, who promised to help her accomplish her goals.

"While you're there, I'll be your mentor, helping from here to keep you on track."

As Morgan, Biz, Tom, and Ruth's children mourned her death, Ruth began integrating back into her nonphysical form.

Your return is welcomed, said Alex.

They will miss me, said Ruth.

Alex agreed. *We never know just when our journey back from physical to nonphysical will come, how or when our pre-incarnate goals will be met. The end is difficult for the physical ones who love us and the ones we love who must stay to accomplish their own goals.*

Morgan took an early ferry to Seattle and picked up Tom Jr. at the airport.

"The big red truck must be part of your new life on the farm. It suits you."

She told him stories about the llamas, ducks, and chickens, avoiding conversation about the accident. Morgan respected his need to hold himself together until he was with his family.

They drove to Ruth and Tom's house in Shoreline where Tom Jr. held his distraught sister, obviously pregnant, as they cried together. He hugged his Aunt Biz and then embraced his father.

"Morgan... I just can't accept that our baby will never know her," Sarah said in a fragile voice as Morgan held her tight, the new life between them.

When Morgan sat beside Biz on the sofa, her friend said, "This sucks," and stared at the wall. "She's all I had. How can I...."

Over the next few days, while Biz sat frozen in grief, Morgan helped Tom make arrangements and greeted neighbors and friends who dropped by with food, flowers, and sympathy. After a small memorial service in the backyard, friends and neighbors left them to their sadness. While Ruth's family lingered in the living room, Tom found Morgan cleaning up the kitchen.

"You got new reading glasses."

"Well, yes, sort of new *reading* glasses," Morgan said with a smile.

Tom handed Morgan an envelope. "I found this on the counter. I guess Ruth never got around to mailing it."

Although Morgan had been wondering about the letter, she couldn't ask. She felt relieved when Tom gave it to her. Morgan could see Ruth standing behind him, smiling, looking content and, Morgan noticed, quite young. Morgan casually put the envelope in her purse, then looked past Tom to make eye contact with Ruth. *We'll miss you*, she said silently to Ruth's hologram.

The next afternoon, she called Yuri from the Bainbridge Island ferry. "I'll be home around seven. Do you want me to pick up anything at Central Market?"

"You sound exhausted. Don't worry, I'll have dinner ready," he said.

She looked at the envelope. *I'll wait until Yuri is with me.* Closing her purse, she got out of the truck. Cold, damp wind whipped her hair into copper cotton candy. She walked toward the back of the ferry. The engines roared and a few people milled about, then began returning to their vehicles as the vessel arrived at the Bainbridge Island dock. She moved through a time warp. *How can the world be the same? Nothing will ever be the same. Ruth is gone. Biz will grow old without her beloved sister, Tom without his wife. Sarah's baby will never know her wonderful grandmother.*

Morgan climbed back into the big red truck. She drove through the dark, across Bainbridge Island, over Agate Pass Bridge, back to her farm and a life that would be different. The ancient Douglas fir invited her under its branches as a big fire beckoned from behind the house.

"This is lovely. The fire's perfect," she said to Yuri as she walked to her favorite chair. "Did the guests check in and out okay?" Howard jumped into her lap and draped himself over her leg.

"They enjoyed the Belgian waffles. I don't think they realized the real inn keeper wasn't here."

"Thank you so much for taking care of the guests, and Howard, and the animals. It's a good thing you were here…. It all seems like part of a plan, doesn't it?" She stroked Howard's soft white fur.

Yuri smiled and handed her a glass of Pinot gris. "Relax while I get your dinner." He went into the house and returned with two plates of grilled salmon, roasted potatoes, and steamed asparagus. He put hers on the wide arm of the Adirondack chair.

"This looks delicious! People brought so much food, but I couldn't eat…. It's nice to be home."

They sat in the dark, comforted by the crackle, glow, and heat from the fire.

"Did you open the envelope?" Yuri finally said.

"No, it's still in my purse. I waited for you. I'm scared."

"What are you scared of?"

"If I knew, I probably wouldn't be scared. It's all so weird. Did Ruth write the letter because the guides asked her to—because they knew there would be an accident? Or did my sassy, irreverent request for proof cause…?"

Yuri walked to the back of her chair. "You understand you had nothing to do with her passing." He put his hands on her shoulders, and she felt his energy coursing through her like revitalizing whirlpool jets.

She patted his hand. "Your energy feels wonderful. Thanks… Intellectually, I know what you're saying is true…, except that's not how it feels."

"The letter will help you. While you get it, I'll put more logs on the fire. You'll feel chilled reading it."

Howard followed her into the house and back to the fire pit, then uncharacteristically curled on the ground beneath her chair.

The envelope contained a letter written on monogrammed stationery. Morgan used a flashlight to read by the fire.

Dearest Morgan and Yuri,…

She looked up at Yuri. "When did you meet Ruth?

"I met her spirit the night of the accident—remember—we were on the blanket watching the stars when Ruth, Sammy, and Alex visited."

"So how did she know to write to you before she left home that day?" Then waving her hand in the air, she said, "Never mind, dumb question."

Morgan zipped up her purple jacket and leaned closer to the fire. Ruth's unique, curly script was unmistakable. Then Morgan realized, through the glasses, the letter had a light of its own:

Dearest Morgan & Yuri,

How are you? I so enjoyed meeting Yuri under the stars, and I'm thrilled that you flowed into each other's lives so naturally. Morgan, you know by now that Yuri has learned to use his sight and intuitive skills. He will teach you about your own skills when you have overcome your fear.

Morgan looked over the top of the glasses. "Yuri, Ruth wrote this before the accident! Before she died! She left this letter on the kitchen counter when she went out that day."

"You asked for proof. I think you got it."

"I have goose bumps and the hair on my arms is standing up," she said.

"Me too," he said. "This is important. Do you realize how lucky we are?"

"Yes, I do," she said quietly, then read on.

Biz will have trouble with my passing. I know you will help her realize that I didn't leave, I just changed form. It's what we do. When Biz comes for a visit, she will be wearing a new cobalt-blue coat. In the pocket, she'll find the necklace we shared as pre-teens. No one else knows that we each wore it to our first boy-girl dance. We thought we lost the locket. I put a new photo of us inside, taken at Sarah's wedding. Please tell her I'm always here if she needs me.

Morgan shook her head, wiped her tears, glanced up at Yuri, then read on.

Spiritual remembering and answers await both of you. Be open to them, and Morgan, don't be afraid. You are ready for Yuri's special talents. He can help you learn to stay connected and trust your instincts. Your maturity and wisdom will teach him as well.

Morgan, thank you for helping my family after the accident. I loved knowing that you could see me. I look forward to visiting soon—my world to your world.

Isn't it wonderful?!

Now you know. Have no more doubts.

Much love,

Your Spiritual Teacher and Eternal Friend,

Ruth

Morgan slowly folded the letter and put it back into the envelope. "Ruth's gone, yet she's not gone. I have the proof I asked for. It's all so difficult to absorb. I feel her love deep, deep inside me. I just don't understand... why... me?"

"It's time to hush that voice in your head."

"Voice?"

"The voice reminding you that you're not worthy of love. You *are* worthy," he said. "It's why you came to the planet. Everyone is worthy of love. As soon as you admit it, we can focus on the next step of your journey."

Morgan pushed the glasses back into her hair. "That unworthy feeling has been inside me all my life. I don't know how to live without it. Guess

I need to quit blaming my parents and take responsibility for my own happiness...." She looked at Yuri's face reflecting the fire's glow. "Right?"

With thoughtful eyes, he held her gaze for a moment... "Can you remember a time in your life when you felt worthy of love?"

"I knew my grandparents loved me."

"Did you feel like you deserved it?"

"I never thought about it," she said.

"Don't think, feel. How did love *feel*… the first time, before the lessons of unworthiness began?"

They sat quietly by the fire. Yuri stirred the coals, added a log, and waited while Morgan closed her eyes and descended into early childhood memories....

Nineteen-month-old Morgan climbed out of her crib, slid down the stairs on a diapered behind, and unhooked the screen door. With the long legs of her too-big hand-me-down PJs dragging in the dewy grass, she toddled to the neighbor's house and knocked on the door.

"Morgan, what are you doing here?" asked the older woman, known in the community as Aunt Bell. "Where's your mommy and daddy?" She peered past Morgan into the still morning air between the two homes.

"Seeping." Morgan slipped under Bell's arm, crossed the linoleum floor, and climbed onto a big chair. "Bell-Bell, I want break-hurst. Let's eat," she said with her little chin and elbows sticking to the oilcloth that protected the oak tabletop.

Bell spread a slice of her homemade bread with butter, sprinkled it with sugar and cinnamon and slid it into the oven. Morgan breathed in the comforting scent. Through her kitchen window, Bell saw Doc wandering in the backyard. "Are you looking for Morgan?" she called out the back door, then with a grandmotherly grin, "She came over for 'break-hurst,'"

"How'd she get out?" asked Doc, rhetorically.

Just then, Mark came bounding down the porch steps, still wearing his pajamas. Anne followed awkwardly, her right hand gripping the rail, her left on her round belly. "Good morning, Aunt Bell," she called. Soft blonde waves cascaded to her shoulders and bright red lips circled a perfect white smile. As she came closer, Anne said in a loud whisper, "Guess what? My water broke! Can you look after Mark and Morgan while we go to the hospital?"

"Of course. Come," she called to Mark. "I'll make you some cinnamon toast."

Morgan's parents had made plans for Aunt Bell to stay with Mark and Morgan when Anne went into labor, but they didn't tell Morgan that a new baby would be joining the family. When Anne's labor started two weeks early, she didn't give Morgan a hug before she left and she didn't tell Morgan that she would be away for a few days. From that day forward, Morgan knew that she no longer deserved her parents' love. Her new sister, Meredith, took Morgan's place in her mother's lap and heart. While Anne looked after her new baby, Bell fed Morgan, read to her, and rocked her while she napped....

⤳

"Bell-Bell loved me no matter what," Morgan told Yuri, "and I knew I deserved it. I never felt like my parents loved me, I wasn't what they wanted but Meredith was, right from the start. Bell-Bell's love for me felt true and right and real and deep. I felt whole in her arms—before my second birthday—and we weren't related. She died about the time I turned five, just as I started school, and learned how to behave like a girl, and Doc started dulling himself with Scotch every night."

"Careful… don't relive your story… go back to Bell-Bell's kitchen, smell the cinnamon. Match the vibration. Feel how it felt to deserve her love. Don't think about it—feel it. Whenever you want to, you can feel loved—and know you deserve love."

chapter twenty-three —
biz meets yuri

*The wiser and more skillful a teacher is,
the more simply and with less artifice
he achieves his ends.*

—Meister Eckhardt

MORGAN STOOD BRUSHING HER TEETH when the phone rang. Even with toothpaste smeared on her lips, she answered in her usual customer service voice. "Morgan Hill Retreat. This is Morgan. How can I help you?"

"Morning, Morgan, Biz here. How are things on the farm?"

"Cold!" she said as she reached for a washcloth. "Yesterday I heated water on the gas stove, then carried buckets out to the chickens and llamas. I felt like a pioneer woman. The power went out for several hours, so the electric gizmos I bought didn't keep their water from freezing... but you didn't call to talk about the animals or the weather. How're you doing?"

"Not so great." Biz's voice trembled, sounding thick and stiff. "I was thinking... if you don't have too many guests... maybe I'd come to the farm for a little break. I need to get out of the city."

"I don't have *any* guests. Come on out. We'll have the place to ourselves. You can go to bed early, sleep in, and I'll serve you breakfast in bed."

"That sounds like heaven. But I don't want you to go to any trouble."

"Not to worry—when are you coming?"

Biz said nothing.

"Hello—Biz? Are you still there? Did we get cut off?"

"Sorry... yes... uh.... I'm here.... Do you have a room ready for tonight?"

"Of course. Will you catch a ferry after work?"

"Well, no." Biz paused for a long moment. "I'm sitting in line right now for the 9:30 a.m. I should be there by 10:30. If you're not ready, I can hang out in Poulsbo."

"That's great! I'm ready. I'll run to the grocery for the basics—you know, coffee, chocolate, ice cream, wine," said Morgan.

"I can stop at Central Market on the way," Biz offered.

"No, no. I need supplies like laundry soap, and toilet bowl cleaner, and I'll get gas for the generator in case the power goes out again. If you get here before I get back, just come on in. I'll leave the front door unlocked. The Sunflower Suite is all ready for you. I'll get the ingredients for that tomato basil tart you liked so much."

"You are the queen of getaway."

"I'm out the door—just make yourself at home. And Biz, I'm so glad you're coming."

Morgan finished brushing her teeth, put on her purple hat and jacket and muddy Uggs, and headed for Central Market.

From the parking lot, she dialed Yuri's cell. "Hi, it's me. Are you having fun with your cousin?"

"We went snowshoeing at Hurricane Ridge. Haven't done that in years. What's up?"

"I just wanted to let you know that my friend Biz, Ruth's sister, is coming to stay for a few days."

"Do you want me to stay away so you two can talk?"

"No, that's not it. Biz needs help with Ruth's death. How will I know if she's ready to hear about the locket?"

"Don't worry, you'll know what to do when the time is right," he assured her. "Do you want me there or not?"

"Yes. No. Maybe. I don't know."

"Be honest. Stop thinking—just feel what you want." He always sounded stern when he guided her to feel rather than think.

"I'd like to have your support... if you don't mind, and I'd love for you to meet Biz."

"How long is she staying?"

"I don't know for sure. I suspect she needs to go back to work on Monday, so she'll probably catch a ferry on Sunday."

"I planned to come back on Sunday morning. That gives the two of you time together, and I'll play it by ear when I get there." Morgan chuckled to herself, 'play it by ear' meant something totally different coming from Yuri. He heard things no one else could hear.

"You're the best! See you Sunday," she said, hanging up the phone. She walked into Central Market while Howard settled into the truck's driver's seat.

Her tires crunched the cold gravel as Morgan drove under the heavy Douglas fir branches. Biz stood at the fence talking to Lars the llama. Ruth's hunter-green Jeep Cherokee, standing in the guest parking area, sent a shiver down Morgan's back. Biz's BMW had been totaled in the accident. She still couldn't make a decision about a new car. Morgan got out of her old truck with a bag of carrots. Howard jumped to the ground, and they joined Biz. "Here's a carrot, if you want to be his friend—just like any man—it's all about food."

They laughed, hugged long and hard, then broke off pieces of carrot for the llamas, both women sniffling. Finally, they carried Biz's bag to the Sunflower Suite. Morgan filled two mugs with steaming Insta-Hot water for tea and began putting groceries away.

"Where's the young man friend? I didn't see his truck."

"He's in Port Townsend visiting his cousin. He'll be back on Sunday." Then she added, "Don't worry, he's good at making himself invisible when I have B&B guests."

"I'm looking forward to meeting him," Biz said in a quiet voice that didn't sound like her. Biz still moved in a surreal vacancy, with no energy inside for dealing with her life.

Morgan handed her friend a mug of fragrant jasmine tea. "I want to be clear. I'm flexible. If you want to be alone for a day or a week or a month, I'll stay out of your way—it's what I do for all of my guests, and Yuri knows the routine. If you want to talk or go for a walk, I'd love to do that too. I know you've got some healing to do, and I want to help any way I can."

"I knew you'd understand. I have to go to work on Monday. I just need a few days to myself, to breathe. Seems like I can't get enough air lately."

Without knowing, Biz had come to the farm for something far more important than solitude. With Yuri's assistance, Biz would begin to see layers of life as if she wore Morgan's glasses.

"I've got paperwork and things to do and there are farm chores, of course. I'll be up in my room or outside if you need me." Morgan gestured to a loaf of bread on the counter. "There are packages of deli roast beef and Cheddar cheese in the fridge. Help yourself when you're hungry, and don't hesitate to let me know if you need anything."

"I think I'll just take a nap or read for a while. I brought Joan Didion's latest book and that book of poetry by Mary Oliver you gave me after your birthday party. Or maybe I'll go outside and talk to the llamas. Do you mind?"

"Are you kidding—the Zen-creatures? Llamas are the most healing animals I've ever met. Sit in the barn and read to them if you want to. They'll love it," Morgan said.

"Let's order pizza for dinner and eat by the fire in the living room. I'll be ready for company by then."

"Perfect," said Morgan. "Pepperoni, mushrooms, and extra cheese, six-thirty-ish."

Morgan put her arms around her friend's thin shoulders, noticing that Biz had lost weight she didn't need to lose. They hugged a long time. Then without further conversation, Biz went to her room and Morgan headed up the stairs, both sniffling again.

Morgan took the opportunity to slow herself down. Paperwork could wait. She opened a closet to find a beautiful cinnamon-colored coverlet and marveled at the effort required to produce it. *Two years ago, this fiber walked the farm on the backs of llamas,* she thought. That spring, Morgan's friend Chela sheared the llamas, then Linda cleaned and carded the fiber and made it into roving that Jan spun into yarn. Marsha used her beautiful loom to weave two coverlets. Morgan had given one to Biz and kept the other. In the summer, while B&B guests slept, Morgan had knitted a scarf and hat for Ruth.

Morgan curled up on the bed with the llama coverlet. Howard snuggled next to her as she reached for a book that had waited on the nightstand for months, *Dance of the Dissident Daughter,* by Sue Monk Kidd, her favorite author. In spite of her interest, she dozed off before the second chapter, with Howard's little body next to her. She didn't wake up until about 3:00 p.m. Relaxed and warm, she dreaded going out into the cold. With the soft coverlet still over her shoulders, and the glasses pushed into her hair, she went down to the kitchen to make tea, thinking, *It's warming up out there, so I'm sure their water is thawed and I filled the feed bins yesterday,* finding any excuse not to go out. Then, through the kitchen window, she noticed Biz sitting on a white plastic lawn chair in the middle of the barn, her feet supported by an overturned red bucket as she read the little book of poetry. Her bright cobalt-blue coat contrasted with the barn's winter shadows. Biz wore a hat and the long cinnamon-brown scarf circled her neck—the same hat and scarf Morgan gave to Ruth after the big birthday party over a year ago. She noticed that Biz had put on the muddy Uggs Morgan usually wore to feed the animals.

As Biz read aloud from Mary Oliver's *House of Light,* the five gentle llamas kushed around her like children in a preschool class. *How do they know she needs them?* Pulling the glasses onto her nose, Morgan saw the holographic figure, clearly Ruth, sitting on the hayloft stairs near Biz. A soft glow flowed like amber smoke among them, from Ruth, from the hat and scarf, from Biz, and from the five llamas, filling the barn with a natural exchange of energetic nourishment. Morgan wished her camera could capture the image of light, color, and shared energy. She knew too well that Biz's fast-paced corporate life left no room to breathe and no time for silence, even though this sort of exchange always lingered just beyond her consciousness. Morgan hoped Ruth's death would help Biz find the silence she needed.

Morgan took a big red mug of tea up to her room, curled up in the coverlet, and got serious about reading her book. A little after six she called to order the pizza.

Just as the Pizza Hut delivery girl pulled into the driveway, Biz emerged from her room.

"There you are. I didn't hear you come in," Morgan said.

"You want beer with your pizza?" Biz asked, opening the fridge.

"Beer sounds perfect."

Biz opened two cold bottles. They served themselves two slices each and moved into the living room. Biz settled into the down-stuffed sofa while Morgan switched on the gas fireplace. "Don't you love gas fireplaces? No muss, no fuss," said Morgan, trying a little too hard to be normal. She sat down on the buff-colored leather chair, with Howard on the ottoman by her feet. They ate pizza, drank beer, and stared at the fire while listening to Sarajane Williams' harp music on the stereo. No conversation was necessary.

Biz stayed in her room most of Saturday while Morgan tended to her animals, answered emails, and managed her business. Again, they sat in silence by the fire after dinner. The old friends quietly read their books. Conversation would have interfered with the delicate violin music that filled the living room even though the stereo was turned off.

Ruth serenaded them.

Morgan was certain Biz heard the music as well but it was still too soon for Biz to see beyond her grief so Morgan said nothing.

Howard jumped off Morgan's lap and left the room. After a while, he returned with the teddy bear he'd played with as a puppy. He jumped onto the sofa, put the teddy in Biz's lap, then sat beside her with his paw on her knee. Biz stroked his soft head and absently moved the dog's toy to the other side of the sofa. Howard put it back in Biz's lap, so Biz took the bear and wiggled it in front of the dog. "Do you want to play with your teddy?"

He took the bear from her and put it back on her lap.

"What's he want?"

"I'm not sure. If you don't want him there, just tell him to get down."

"Oh, he's fine, sort of comforting really." She smoothed Howard's soft white fur and took a long, jagged breath. "I miss her so much."

"I know you do. So do I." Morgan hesitated. "Sometimes I feel like she's here."

"Me too!" said Biz, glad Morgan said it first. "This afternoon, I put on that llama-wool scarf you knitted for her and I thought I felt her in the barn with me. I even heard her playing the violin… I guess it's just my grief."

"Maybe she was with you."

Biz stood, walked nervously to the kitchen. "You want another slice?"

"No thanks. I think I'll take Howard for a walk in the moonlight, if you'll come with."

"Great idea. Looks like a full moon and no cloud cover. I'll get my coat."

Morgan dropped the teddy bear into Howard's toy basket as they went out the back door.

The llamas danced anxiously as the two women and the little dog walked toward the fence.

"Look!" said Biz, pointing. "Howard's so white he's glowing in the moonlight."

Morgan had noticed his glow before, even without the moonlight.

The moon cast a deep shadow beneath the dogwood tree as they walked to the lavender bed.

Biz said, "This is gorgeous, it's as bright as daylight." Soft moonlit puffs billowed like spinnakers with each breath. "Ruth loves to walk in moonlight…. I mean…," Biz whispered, "she did…."

~

The next day, Yuri's truck pulled into the drive as Morgan and Biz lingered over coffee; Biz, wearing one of the inn's spa robes and Morgan in her red polar fleece bathrobe.

Biz stood. "I better get dressed."

"No need to rush off. He'll hang out in his trailer until you're ready to meet him."

"It's past one o'clock already," she said but sat back down.

"Can't you take tomorrow off? You *are* the owner, after all."

"You know, I think I will." She stood up again. "I'll send an email to my admin and tell her to reschedule everything on tomorrow's calendar. Then I'll take a nap and read in my room. Can we all have dinner together?"

"Sure! I'll ask Yuri if he wants to cook for us."

"You are a lucky girl." Biz hugged Morgan, then walked to her room.

Morgan stepped out the back door and met Yuri as he headed his trailer. "You don't need to hide out. Biz went back to her room. And she's staying until tomorrow. Would you mind fixing dinner for us all?"

"I have groceries in the truck."

"Of course you do," she smiled.

"Seemed like a pot roast and potatoes kind of day," he said.

"You're wonderful," she said, giving him a hug. "Glad you're back. Now, I need to get dressed and feed the animals."

While Morgan managed farm chores and Biz napped, Yuri browned the roast in the Dutch oven, then added potatoes, onions, and carrots. He poured Merlot over the roast, poured a glass for himself, then slid the red enameled pot into the oven at 325 degrees.

His big, callused hands tore romaine lettuce into bite-size pieces. Then he sliced mushrooms, red peppers, and cucumber into thin slices and arranged the vegetables in a big wooden bowl. For the dressing, he liquefied slices of fresh ginger with fresh-squeezed lemon juice, added a garlic clove, and a dash of salt and cayenne pepper. The kitchen filled with the mingled aromas of garlic, ginger, and lemon as he slowly poured a stream of olive oil in the Cuisinart, then transferred the mixture to a Mason jar.

After putting the salad in the fridge, he stood by the kitchen window sipping wine, and watching Morgan talk to Lars. Something about her—the way she walked, her constant smile, her hair, the way she loved her animals. He felt warm and at home with her.

Yuri walked toward the pasture. "Are you finished with the wheelbarrow?"

She pointed to the back of the house. "I put it next to the woodpile."

"Perfect. Thanks."

Morgan gathered eggs, then joined Yuri by the fire pit. "I only got two green eggs today." Her basket held six eggs in assorted colors and sizes. "The Araucanas don't like the cold, even with the heat lamp in the coop 24/7. The Marans are worse, not one dark-brown egg. Betty Bantam is still laying her tiny egg, and fortunately, the Wyandottes and Orpingtons are happy in cold weather."

Yuri looked up as he started the fire. "I have no idea what you just said."

She laughed. "Sorry, I forget. Not everyone is as enamored with chickens as I am."

"All I know is, I've never tasted a better egg."

"I feed them soy-free organic food I get from a farmer in Kingston."

"There you go again," he teased.

"Sorry—I didn't mean to bore you with chicken information," she laughed.

He smiled. "I enjoy your excitement and passion—even about chickens. If everyone cared about their food the way you care about those chickens, we'd all live to one hundred and fifty."

Biz walked from the house to the fire pit with her llama coverlet draped over the bright blue coat. "I thought I heard you laughing out here. The house smells so good!"

"Come meet the cook. Biz, I'd like to present Dr. Yuri Bozek. Yuri, this is my longtime and dear friend, Elizabeth Bennett."

He extended his big hand to her. "Nice to meet you, Elizabeth. You have quite the literary name."

"As you might guess, my mother loved Jane Austen. And she had a great sense of humor. Please, call me Biz."

Morgan said, "You want to sit out here or go back in the house?"

"Is it too early for a glass of wine by the fire?" asked Biz.

Morgan smiled, thinking, *this is a good sign. She's never had a glass of wine before five o'clock in her entire life.*

"You ladies stay here by the fire—I'll get you some wine. White or red? I bought both."

"White, please," they said in unison, then laughed. Morgan caught a brief glimpse of the happier Biz she once knew.

Yuri returned to the fire pit balancing a tray with two stemless glasses of Pinot gris, one Merlot, a log of organic goat cheese rolled in fresh herbs, and a basket of gourmet wheat crackers.

"That looks wonderful," said Morgan. "You know how much I love goat cheese."

"You carry that tray like you've had experience," said Biz.

"I worked as a waiter when I was in college."

"Where did you go to school?"

"I studied psychology at Arizona State."

"My sister Ruth studied music at Arizona State."

"You must miss your sister," he said in a voice that could calm a hurricane.

There it is, Morgan thought. *It took him less than sixty seconds to get her to talk about Ruth.*

Biz's usual high-speed persona melted away. She responded to Yuri's energy like stepping into a well-worn pair of bedroom slippers. "That's why I came to visit Morgan for a few days. I can't cope with her death. I thought going back to work would help, but I can't concentrate—I'm worthless. I sat in a client meeting the other day and I had no idea what went on. I miss her so much…. How will I grow old without her?"

Biz took a long, shuddering breath, and the tears finally started flowing.

Morgan and Yuri sipped their wine while Biz wept.

"That's good," he said. "You need to cry, allow the pain."

While Yuri sat quietly with Biz. Morgan carried her egg basket into the house.

She peeked in the oven, releasing the aroma of roasting beef, onions, and vegetables. The aroma reminded her of Grandma's kitchen at harvest time, and… something just beyond her memory….

After washing her hands, she set the table with a soft sage-green tablecloth, cloth napkins, and the white dishes she bought in Hong Kong.

Howard followed Morgan to her room. She put on the glasses and throw the llama coverlet over her purple fleece coat, then joined Biz and Yuri by the fire pit. Howard jumped into her lap.

Biz didn't notice Morgan had left. "I never appreciated Ruth's tarot readings," Biz told Yuri. "She pulled cards from a deck and told people what their lives were all about."

"Have you thought about how she knew what the tarot cards meant?"

"Now I realize she must have been more aware—more tuned in with the world than the rest of us." Biz paused, "Like you are, Yuri."

"Do you think anyone can learn to *tune in*—as you call it?"

"I used to think all that woo-woo stuff was silly," Biz said. "Now, not so much. Wouldn't it be wonderful if we could all..." Her voice trailed off into the dimming winter twilight.

Yuri felt Biz's growing trust and her openness to accept almost any kind of help. "Can we try something?" Yuri asked.

"Sure."

"Stand up....Now, tell me how you feel."

"I've been feeling weird since the accident." Biz wiggled her arms and twisted her neck. "Like my body is in one place and my mind is in another. I can't relax."

"It's good you're aware of it. Now, think about walking in the moonlight and let your mind empty." The sun disappeared behind the Olympic Mountains, and a hazy pink twilight surrounded them.

Biz stood by the fire. "Should I close my eyes?"

"If you want... Just breathe comfortably.... Now, try breathing in for the count of five, hold for the count of five, release for the count of five, then count to five before you inhale again. Just keep breathing for a few minutes."

He waited, then asked, "Do you know where your energy is?"

"Do I have energy?"

"Everyone does. Imagine that your energy is flowing from the top of your head, through your body and the soles of your feet, down to the center of the earth.... Don't forget to breathe... Just clear your mind...."

Yuri stood behind Biz, using his energy to calm her. In normal circumstances, he would teach her techniques to feel safe and connected with her body. However, because of her sorrow, he assisted her with his own energy, moving his palms in circles behind Biz's lower back. Morgan watched clear magenta light absorb into the base of Biz's spine.

Biz said, "I don't know what you're doing back there, but I'm starting to feel better, like my feet are on the ground for the first time since... the accident. It's comforting."

Yuri looked at Morgan's face, glowing in reflected firelight.

She smiled at him, *Thank you.* She felt grateful for his willingness, eagerness, to help her grief-stricken friend. She knew that, essentially, he was doing her an important favor as well.

"I'm glad you feel comforted. Stay relaxed and enjoy that feeling for a few minutes while you continue to breathe to the count of five," Yuri told Biz. He slowly stepped away, stirred the coals, and added logs. "Are you ready for something more?"

"Do I have to stop?"

"Absolutely not. You can feel this grounded sensation any time you want to, even at the office." He stood beside her chair. "You might want to sit down for the next exercise. Morgan, you can do it too if you want."

Biz looked at Morgan, startled, as if her friend had just arrived from the moon.

"It's okay, Biz. Yuri and I did these exercises when he first arrived. If you'd rather have privacy while Yuri helps you, I can go inside and leave the two of you alone. I don't mind at all. I can—" she started to stand.

"No no no, it's fine. Stay. I just, well...I just...it felt weird. I forgot where I was for a minute." She walked around the fire pit, shook her arms, and sipped her wine, trying to regain her usual control. "What's next?"

"Don't lose the feeling. Just breathe comfortably." He waited until she sat down. "Put your hands in front of you as though you're holding a small melon with both hands.... Good. Now let your eyes go out of focus while you stare at the space between your palms."

They sat in silence for several minutes while Morgan and Biz stared.

"Woo-who, what's that light? Oh rats, it's gone."

"If you think too much, the energy will vanish. Just stare at the space, out of focus, and let your mind go blank."

Biz found this even more difficult than Morgan had when Yuri first taught her. Several times, she stood up, walked around the fire, then sat down and tried again.

Morgan enjoyed the purple orb she seemed to be holding in her palms. She had moved beyond the need to understand the energy that caused it. She thought the glasses allowed her to see the light so easily. When she realized the glasses were still perched in her hair, the light vanished.

I did it without the glasses! She thought.

Yuri enjoyed goat cheese and crackers while Biz and Morgan practiced creating the light between their palms.

Finally, Biz said, "Is that roast ready? I'm hungry."

"Wow! Great meal. Where did you learn to cook?" Biz asked Yuri as she took the last bite of potato.

"I got promoted to sous chef at the restaurant in Tempe."

"What? You never mentioned that before—no wonder our meals are so wonderful," marveled Morgan. "You're not a lumberjack or a professor—you're a chef!"

"Those things and more, I guess," he said.

"More indeed," said Biz. "Thanks for your help tonight, Yuri. Morgan told me you weren't like other men. I didn't understand what she meant until tonight."

"Are you ready for another session?"

Biz hesitated, then waved, "Why not? But first I'll help clean up."

"No you won't." Morgan began to clear the table. "Yuri and I have a deal. He cooks, I clean up, and guests just enjoy the place." She looked across the table at Yuri. "Of course, when I made the deal I didn't know he was a professional chef. I sure lucked out."

After cleaning up the kitchen, Morgan found Biz sitting on the bench by the fire. Her eyes were closed and Yuri stood behind her. His huge hands rested on her shoulders, directing energy from the universe as if the light of the moon had come to earth to help. Biz absorbed the glow like a thirsty pasture in summer rain.

On Monday morning, Yuri stayed in the trailer, writing, while Biz and Morgan had coffee. They took a long walk in the tree farm and returned to find him in the kitchen making waffles.

"I'm going to gain ten pounds while I'm here," said Biz.

"It wouldn't hurt if you did," said Morgan. "You're thinner than you've ever been."

"I know. I look more like Mom."

"How did you sleep?" asked Yuri.

"Better than I have in a long time, and especially since Ruth's accident."

"I like your blue coat," said Yuri, glancing at Morgan. He knew that Biz wasn't emotionally ready to hear about the letter Ruth wrote before the accident, but finding the locket would help her understand that Ruth remained nearby.

"Thanks. I got it a few days ago. I needed something to brighten up this dark winter."

Morgan and Yuri made eye contact. *Do you want me to tell her?* he asked telepathically.

Morgan nodded with an appreciative smile.

"Check the right pocket; Ruth put something there for you," said Yuri.

"She couldn't have. I just bought this coat." Biz put her right hand in the pocket and pulled out the necklace. "What's going on? This looks like the locket..."

"You and Ruth shared?" he said.

"I thought we... lost it."

"It's the locket you each wore to your first boy-girl dance," he said.

"No one else in the world knew about the locket, not even Mom. It was our secret. How could you know...? How could Ruth...?"

"Ruth put a new photo inside, the two of you at Sarah's wedding," Yuri told her.

As Biz opened the locket, Morgan held her elbow to guide her into a chair.

"Ruth loves you very much and wants you to know she's always with you, even now," Yuri said while serving Belgian waffles with fresh strawberries as if nothing had happened.

After Biz left, Morgan found an envelope in the guest room. On the outside, Biz had written: *Yuri cooked, Morgan did the dishes, and I behaved like a guest.* Inside Morgan found cash to cover lodging for three nights and a note:

Dear Morgan and Yuri,
There are no words.
I am so grateful.
Know that you are treasured.
Love,
Biz

chapter twenty-four – let it go

Feel the feeling and drop the story.
—Pema Chödrön, Buddhist nun

"You look angry," Yuri said, chopping vegetables for a stir-fry while Morgan set the table.

"That woman treated me like crap. She knew checkout was 11:00 a.m. but she stayed all afternoon, then had a fit when I charged her the late checkout fee. I work my ass off to keep this place in five-star condition but she found things to complain about. Her robe was too big, the towels were too soft, and the jets in the tub were too noisy. She didn't tell me she wanted a vegan breakfast and then got nasty because I served eggs. I distinctly remember telling her when she booked that my hens lay great eggs. She didn't say a word. I even asked her if she had any food issues and she said no. This morning she told me that being vegan is not a 'food issue.' She treated me like the help. I hate it. Where do people get off, behaving like that?"

"Her nastiness isn't your problem, it's hers."

"Then why do I feel like crap?"

"Because you let her upset you," he said.

"I try to put up a wall around myself, but they still get to me."

"The same wall you've been hiding behind your whole life?"

Morgan dropped a spoon. "Wow, you don't hold back." She slammed the silverware drawer with her hip.

"Just let it pass through."

"You make it sound so flippin' easy! Okay, so I try to block out bad feelings. Is that such a bad thing?"

"Not if you like getting upset by disrespectful people," he said in a calm quiet voice.

Morgan walked into the living room and flopped onto the sofa.

Yuri followed.

"I need a minute to think about what you said." She took a deep breath, and he waited. "How do I let it go through instead of trying to block the feelings?"

He smiled as he sat down on the leather chair across from her with his elbows on his knees.

"Please don't say, 'you tell me,'" she said.

He just shrugged his big shoulders and grinned.

Morgan shook her head, still irritated. "Okay…just feel the feeling, acknowledge it, determine that it's not my issue, and let it go."

"You *do* know how."

"I suppose… it feels like a technique I used to deal with my ex-husband, just before I filed for divorce. I read about it in a book by Wayne Dyer… changed my life. Once I realized Paul couldn't make me feel bad if I didn't let him, he never controlled me again."

"Same technique."

"You teach me something new every day—in spite of myself."

"You already knew," he said. "I just helped you reposition."

She tried to imagine the woman's nastiness passing through her. It wasn't as difficult as she thought. The energy didn't belong to her. Soon she felt normal again.

"When did you divorce?" Yuri said.

"1980."

"You've been single a long time. Do you want to be married again?"

"For a long time I wanted to. Now I know that if I'd married any of the men I dated, I'd have divorced again. I've changed—become a different person. Back then, I was *The Runaway Bride*. Did you ever see that movie?"

"Julia Roberts and Richard Gere?"

"Yes. Every time she met a man, she ate what he liked to eat, did what he liked to do, like a Dusty Springfield song from the Sixties."

He looked at her blankly.

"Sorry, sometimes I forget how young you are. Anyway, in the movie, she never thought about what *she* wanted. That's how I was. I didn't have a clue what I liked, so I waited to see what he liked and that's what I liked too. Now I know better. Now I'm so independent, I don't think I could tolerate having a man around all the time. ALL the time. I'm surprised how easy it's been having you here." Then she laughed, "Of course, you sleep in the trailer. That helps." She joked but it was true. If he lurked underfoot 24/7, their relationship would be vastly different. "How about you? I never asked if you ever got married."

"Never did."

"A sexy guy like you? How did you get away? Women must be all over you." Morgan stood up, flipped the switch on the living room fireplace, then sat down again.

"Remember I told you about Q-Zee?"

"The housekeeper's daughter?"

"I fell in love with her. We dated in high school, but my parents didn't like the idea."

"That sounds like a movie too. Audrey Hepburn and Humphrey Bogart."

"About the time I graduated from high school, Mrs. Hanover remarried and they moved to the East Coast. I tried to stay in touch from Arizona State, but Q-Zee met a lawyer in D.C. The last time I heard from her, she was happily married with two kids and another on the way. Q-Zee had no idea how I felt. I think my parents had something to do with keeping her away from me. They wanted to be sure that I got an education. I went to school in Russia for a couple of years to study language and physics. Dad wanted me to be able to read his Russian books."

"Wait, you mean you speak and read Russian and studied physics—in Russian? Geez, Yuri!"

He shrugged. "Grandpa taught me Russian, and Dad made sure I didn't forget. Anyway, after I got back, I tried dating girls I met at school. The scenario was always the same. She would start asking relationship questions, and I would feel smothered." He shook his head. "Even after Q-Zee lost her memory of the colored light, I knew that somewhere inside, her awareness was still there."

"You studied psychology and physics and never met people you could talk to?"

"My metaphysical world scares people, especially scientists. I have a small circle of *awake* friends I stay in touch with. I find, however, I'd rather be alone with the spirits than socialize with people who walk around asleep all the time."

"I think that's why running this bed and breakfast is getting more difficult for me. I have to be nice to people, even the nasty ones. Sometimes I don't feel like being friendly even to the nice ones. I just want to hide until they go away."

"Maybe that's why you aren't getting the bookings you think you want."

"What do you mean—*think I want*? I'm doing all kinds of marketing; it's the economy, not me."

"You're a powerful manifestor, Morgan. If you wanted people in your house all the time, they'd be here. I think your true intent prevents bookings rather than attracts them."

"Wow, I never thought of that.... So now what do I do? I've got this property I need to maintain and no income unless I get bookings that I probably don't want."

"Either change how you feel about customers or sell the place."

"When I spent all that money remodeling, I thought if I got tired of inn keeping, I could sell it but I'll never find a buyer in this market."

"Not with that attitude."

～

A cashmere-colored Jaguar drove under the Douglas fir tree, beyond the *GUEST PARKING* sign, and stopped next to the two red Chevy pickups. Morgan dumped the scoop of llama manure onto the compost pile and walked to the fence as she pulled the glasses onto her face. *If these people have a reservation, they're three hours early and they didn't park in the guest parking area. But no guests are booked...,* she thought.

"Hi, Morgan," said her sister, Meredith, floating toward the fence as if preforming *glissade en avant en pointe*. Turquoise and magenta silk billowed behind her. Her long graying-blonde hair stretched smoothly into a tight bun at the back of her head. "How do you like *my* new car?"

Her voice felt like leafless oak branches abrading a cold windowpane.

A tall man emerged from the passenger's seat, impeccably dressed in Ralph Lauren sports clothes that had never seen sweat. He looked like Jeff Goldblum, with gray hair, olive skin, and bulgy eyes. His huge, awning-like nose shaded full lips and a nervous grin. Morgan guessed he was near seventy, about ten years older than Meredith. His gray, nearly colorless aura hugged close to his thin figure and felt sad and timid, as if captive.

"Hi Mer," said Morgan, swallowing her surprise. Meredith's fortune resulted from divorcing her first two husbands. She never worked a day in her life. "The Jag is beautiful." Cautiously, she added, "I had no idea you were coming by today."

"What are you doing with that little rake?" said Meredith, her nose wrinkling. "Don't you have people to muck the pastures?"

"No, I do most of the work here myself, inside and out."

"Well, anyway... we decided to surprise you. I told Carl I knew a B&B where we could celebrate our engagement, so we hopped onto the Kingston ferry." Meredith made no effort to introduce Carl who remained a step behind, fidgeting with his hat.

The llamas lined up by the fence, two on one side of Morgan, three on the other, as if ready to defend their master if necessary. "Congrats on the engagement. But I'm sorry, Mer, I'm not ready for guests tonight," said Morgan. Meredith had been engaged many times, so the occasion held no glitter. The thought of having Meredith and this stranger in her house overnight made Morgan's stomach hurt. She stayed behind the fence. "You should have called."

"Well...I suppose we can come back next weekend. You aren't booked, are you?" said Meredith, her tone dismissive.

Morgan took a deep breath and made a decision. In the past, she would have avoided a confrontation at any cost, allowing Meredith and her fiancé to spend the night, unannounced, even if she had to spend the rest of the day getting the guest room ready or turn away paying guests. No more. Morgan would not allow Meredith to invade the inn's tranquility, but she couldn't just say *I don't want you in my house.* "The spring season hasn't picked up yet…but…Mer, this is how I make a living now."

Meredith's face flushed and her back stiffened. Carl took an involuntary step back. "You made all that money as a hotshot international VP, you can afford to let us stay at your stupid B&B." She was accustomed to getting her own way.

The air stung like shards of glass when Meredith spewed her negativity. They both knew it had nothing to do with money.

"You can't just show up and expect me to fix your breakfast, clean up after you, and turn away paying guests. It has nothing to do with what I can or cannot afford. It has to do with respect."

In a low, eerie voice, Meredith said, "Respect? What the hell do *you* know about respect? You never respected me or our family. You didn't even come to Daddy's memorial."

"Doc wouldn't care, even if he knew. Anyway, you've often told me how much you don't like me. Why did you come here?"

"We wanted to tell you that we're engaged, but you…you can forget about coming to our wedding!" She turned on her delicate platform heel, and stomped towards the car. To Carl she said, "I told you my sister's a bitch."

Still safely behind the fence, Morgan and the llamas watched Meredith and Carl climb into the Jaguar. The animals returned to grazing while Morgan leaned on the fence and took another deep breath. The weight of her sister's negativity lifted, and she realized that Meredith could no longer make her feel inadequate or responsible.

Yuri joined Morgan as she closed the gate behind her. "Lunch is ready. Hope you like tuna fish sandwiches," said Yuri, watching the Jag turn out of the driveway. "Nice car. Did you know those people?"

"My sister Meredith and her fiancé planned to spend the night—without calling ahead. I said no and she freaked out. Is it possible for people to be born evil?"

"What do you mean?"

"Her aura is weird. I never noticed without the glasses. The color is a menacing deep taupe with streaks of maroon and midnight blue, nearly black." Morgan shivered involuntarily.

"I don't know that she's evil, she's probably just out of touch with her higher Self, living at the lowest level of human consciousness." He thought for a moment. "I've always focused my studies on the higher levels, avoiding the negativity of people like her, so I'm no expert. How do you feel?"

"I'm fine. Great, really. She didn't get to me like she used to."

chapter twenty-five – do re mi

ONE AFTERNOON IN APRIL, AS MORGAN FED THE ANIMALS, she heard music and noticed the open hayloft window. She threw a scoop of cracked corn for the chickens to scratch and found Yuri in the hayloft playing his balalaika. Sunlight reflected off the big holy tree by the fence, giving the dimly lit loft a greenish glow.

"There's something about a big lumberjack playing a balalaika in my barn that seems totally normal," she teased. "Even the chickens and llamas enjoy your music."

"I finished mowing. Do you have time to sit down before dinner?"

"Sure, everything's ready for the guests tomorrow." She climbed onto a hay bale.

"Remember when you saw the light from our energy centers?"

"I'll never forget," she said softly as she put her hands behind her head and leaned back on another bale of hay.

"There's more…"

"There's always more, Yuri."

"Can you do the breathing to the count of five like we did that night? In… Out…"

Morgan breathed deeply and quickly relaxed into the aroma of fresh-cut grass mixed with the scent of hay.

"Now, I'm going to play a note, and I want you to tell me what happens. Ready?"

She nodded.

He plucked an F and sang, "Fa." then, "Tell me what you feel."

"I don't feel anything," she shrugged.

"Then why did you put your hand on your heart?"

She looked down as if her hand had found its way there on its own. She smiled up at him. "Cool."

"Just breathe, and we'll see if my intention can influence your actions."

Her hand quickly lifted to her forehead, the third eye, as he plucked a chord. "I could feel it, even before you did anything!"

"Before I played the frequency that resonated closely with your intuitive center, I gave it a boost with my own energy, so it worked faster. It's similar to the way I helped Biz after Ruth died. She couldn't relax so I helped her feel safe and reconnected to her body by energetically stimulating her first major energy organ at the bottom of her spine. I wouldn't do it without permission, though."

"So the third eye is the chakra or *energy organ* for intuition. That makes sense. When I first started wearing these glasses, I had headaches so I had my eyes checked. The doctor said the prescription in the glasses was perfect for me."

"Do you understand why your head ached?"

"Is it like working out at the gym for the first time in months? As if my energy *muscles* were out of shape? My eyes were fine but the third eye worked overtime?"

"I wouldn't say *as if*. Your intuition began to engage and it caused some actual discomfort. Do you still have headaches when you wear the glasses?"

"Just when I'm trying hard to understand some of the things you talk about."

"Ah, I'm doing my job," he smiled.

Then, with a mischievous grin, he played a D chord.

Morgan jumped up, onto a bale of hay. "That orange glow and those butterflies—down there!"

He laughed. "See how the vibration matched the energy center? Nobody touched you physically, but you felt it. Right?"

"Yes...! I...! did!" Thinking, *a dildo would have been less effective.*

"The energy center and the physical body's functionality combine to cause a physical sensation. What does the smell of cinnamon do for you?"

"I feel warm and loved." Without thinking, she put her hand on her heart as she settled back onto the hay.

"Do you know why?"

"Cinnamon has always been a comforting fragrance for me but I didn't realize why until the other night when I remembered cinnamon toast at Bell-Bell's. It smells like love and comfort and belonging."

"What about your financial concerns? How do you feel when you pay your bills?"

Morgan put her hand on her stomach.

"Feel what happened in your body?" he asked.

"My stomach started to feel weird and the warmth in my heart went away."

"Western medicine ignores the energy organs, as if everything can be corrected with drugs and surgery. I'm certain there's more to healing than Western medical science would have us believe. It doesn't help that the medical industry is a financial behemoth." He played a tune and looked at her again. "As I said, we're spirit in physical form, not the other way around. Some studies show that sixty percent of what we experience comes from our eyes. That can't be right. So much more comes from the other senses and the energy organs that connect us to the universe and to each other."

He played another tune while Morgan relaxed on the hay. Then he plucked and sang, "Do Re Mi Fa So La Ti Do." A rainbow of color arched between them in the greenish haze.

"That's eight, I thought there were seven chakras—excuse me—energy centers? Organs? I don't know what words to use."

"Use any word that works: chakra, center, vortex, structure. Just know what it means to you. There's an eighth center over the head, impacting all the others. It brings the other seven centers into a cohesive whole. Like the difference between a field scattered with stones and the unified structure of a *cairn*[10]." His tone was soft and his vocal cadence gave Morgan time to absorb his coaching. "There are actually two more above that. The ratio of physicality to energetic alignment diminishes as you move up the body. The base center is about eighty percent physical and twenty percent energy. At the crown it's closer to twenty percent physical and eighty percent energy. There are three above the crown, until you get to ninety-nine percent energy at the tenth level. These ten structures project physicality from the nonphysical."

She looked confused. "Sorry, Dr. Bozek, you lost me, 'project physicality from the nonphysical?'"

"You are a spirit with a body, not a body with a spirit."

"That shifts the familiar paradigm." She knew he had said this many times since he arrived but it finally made sense to her. "How do you know all this?"

"I saw and felt the structure, even as a small child."

"Like the time you and Q-Zee made colored light in the dark closet?"

"Exactly. In college, I studied different cultures' understanding of spiritual phenomena. For example, the term *spiritual energy*. The Chinese call it *qi* or *chi*; the Japanese call it *ki*, and in India it's *prana*."

"Of course! That's the *ki* in *reiki*. I remember Ruth talking about that."

"Each term roughly translates to *breath* or *energy* or *air*, but it's all very intangible because each person feels the energy or the sensation differently—even within the same culture. Because of my parents, I had access to some of the most unusual materials on the planet. I spent hours in library stacks studying books that still aren't available on the Internet, some of them in Russian. The Internet uses metaphysical jargon, and the information is often misleading. Our vocabulary fails to describe the inherent individuality of metaphysical phenomena. A good example of this individuality is how you see your guides."

"What do you mean? You see your guides too."

"Yes, but you see them as genderless."

"They are," she insisted.

"To you they're genderless because you have gender issues."

---

10   **cairn** - *a pile of stones marking a landmark, trail, memorial, etc. used all over the globe since prehistoric times.*

"I don't have *gender issues*." Morgan felt the anger rise to her throat.

"When was the last time you had a loving relationship with a man?"

"Wow, you don't hold back, do you?" She jumped off the bale of hay and leaned facing the wall by the window with both arms stretched over her head. He waited for her to move beyond her anger, until she could think clearly about what he meant. No words were necessary.

As she paced between the stacks of hay bales, she said, "My father and my husband saw women as servants. Then, when I escaped that, I ran into *gender issues*, as you call it, at the office. I had a boss who patted my butt and told me I was his favorite. I bet no boss of yours ever did that. All the boy/girl crap drives me insane!"

"So you admit you're negatively influenced when it comes to gender."

Pacing back and forth in the hayloft she said, "Yes, I guess, if that's what you mean. As a kid, I preferred being outdoors working in the yard but my chores were always inside because I was a girl. My brother had to weed the garden. Now he wishes he could have learned to cook. I wanted to work with wood, but Mom insisted I learn to knit. *Gender issues* aren't unique to people my age."

"Your ego is making you defensive. Just let it go. Breathe." He gave her time to move beyond her ego. "If you saw your guide Sammy as either male or female, you'd relate differently to his/her advice and guidance. You would feel it differently in your body and hear it differently in your mind."

Finally, she climbed back onto the hay bale and leaned back. "I don't like it, but I see what you mean."

"All of us see and feel our environment based on what we came to the planet to learn, I call it *inherent individuality*. Sometimes the lessons are unpleasant. My energy amplifies and accelerates your growth, making you uncomfortable. It's understandable." He played a short tune on the balalaika, harmonizing with the swallows as they floated in the sunlight beyond the barn door.

Easing away from the gender discussion, Yuri said, "There are broader issues as well. For example, some people see specific colors and hear specific sounds associated with the energy organs. Words like *chakra, energy, chi,* and *quantum* become jargon. And jargon is isolating and provides a narrow view, particularly when teachers or experts use it. The words become dogma, because that's the prevailing model of spiritual communication. It's how most people relate. They can't see what they're doing."

Morgan stared at him and wondered if she would ever know who he really was.

"Are you familiar with the healing powers of harp music?" he asked.

"Sure. It's great when I'm trying to get in touch with a feeling or something I can't explain. Sometimes it's happy and sometimes it makes me cry," she said.

He looked at her intently, his eyes narrowed. "I think it's because you remember things associated with the harp."

"Remember? No one I know plays the harp. I've only recently discovered how much I love it. Last summer I listened to an album—I mean CD—you know, music on my MP3—when I mowed the yard."

"Since you found the glasses?" He looked at the glasses tucked into her copper and silver curls.

She nodded and pulled them onto her face and the greenish aura of Yuri's balalaika appeared. "Did you take lessons on your balalaika?"

"Not really. I found this one in an antique store in Kiev when I was twelve. I picked it up and started playing, so Mom bought it for me. She thought I was a musical genius. I have newer one at home."

"How did you learn the songs you play?"

"I'm sure I remember from another lifetime, just as you play the harp."

"Well, you play the balalaika beautifully. Your touch makes it lovely, the music swirls around you, amplifying your soul." She put her hand on her heart and took a deep breath. "I shiver the same way when I hear a harp played with heart. I felt the same sensation when Ruth played her violin."

He played a familiar tune and again the rainbow of colors appeared between them, with a twinkling white glow above their heads, as if their souls whispered.

She leaned back in the hay. "Don't stop."

"A month ago you would have gone running out of here."

"I've grown."

"After dinner, let's play a duet in the attic," he said.

chapter twenty-six — the catacombs

The minute I heard my first love story,
I started looking for you,
not knowing how blind that was.
Lovers don't finally meet somewhere.
They're in each other all along.

Rumi, *The Illuminated Rumi*

MORGAN SPREAD THE QUILT ON THE ATTIC FLOOR as Yuri lit candles and set peat smoking in abalone shells. The attic filled with flickering light and earthy fragrance.

As a full moon appeared on the horizon, casting long shadows behind trees and beyond creatures, they inhaled the silence, the memories, then began their string duet.

Oddly familiar tunes mixed in harmonic union with the scent of wax and smoke while orbs of colored light danced in the rafters. Ancestral musicians joined them in a harmonious celebration of awakened gratitude and joy.

Collective memory unfolded before them....

Nomads, dressed in hand-spun fabrics and tanned hides, drove their small herd of long-horned aurochs southward for warm winter grazing. Teams of Percheron draft horses pulled wagons loaded with bread and vegetables, pottery, finely woven wool fabrics, musical instruments, and other for-trade goods.

The Healers stayed behind, stowing their abundant harvest in underground cellars: potatoes, carrots, apples, nuts, cabbage, beets, corn, and grains. Frozen rabbit, beef and cured wild boar were stored in a chamber just below the surface.

For centuries of winters, fat-burning lanterns illuminated the chambers and covered the ceilings with sticky black soot.

Some Healers spent each winter sculpting clay they fired in ovens. Others were skilled at carving wood, weaving, or etching petroglyphs on the cave walls. Only the rise and fall of the tidal thermal pool marked the daily passing of winter's time.

Women and men shared culinary duties: grinding corn and grains, making bread, and preparing borsch[11], goluptsi[12], vareniky[13], and deruny.

The Healers respected one another, honoring vital frequencies and the unique terrestrial talents of each community member. Competition, social hierarchy, and gender-assigned roles remained unnecessary and as uncommon as a warm, tropical breeze.

Their community enjoyed a life of consciousness with fully integrated essence. Ancestral spirit guides moved among them, sharing ancient wisdom. They developed a written language and documented their spiritual knowledge on paper they made from tree pulp. Ink was rendered from ground walnut shells, soot, and fermented leaves.

Nomads returned with the summer sunlight, their teams of horses pulling wagons piled high with supplies. Calves and colts frolicked alongside. Salt for curing meat was hauled along with bundles of unusual timbers for the artisans to carve into idols, bowls, drums, and flutes. One wagon hauled heavy barrels of beach sand from the Black Sea. The Healers mixed the sand with ground volcanic rock and learned to smelt steel to make tools for preparing food, tanning hide, and woodcarving.

Skilled artisans melted sand in huge vats in a deep rock kiln and learned to blow glass. They designed metal rods and tubes for blowing the molten

---

11   **borsch** - *soup made with beetroot, giving it a deep reddish-purple color.*

12   **goluptsi** - *cabbage stuffed with meat and cooked in tomato-based sauce.*

13   **vareniky** - *a boiled half-circled dumpling stuffed with cottage cheese, potatoes, and meat.*

mixture and wooden paddles to help form the blown glass into smooth, colorful orbs and vessels.

They experimented with strings they made from cattle and rabbit gut and fashioned the clàrsach and balalaika. Sweet musical tunes rippled through the catacombs during gratitude ceremonies deep in sacred chambers, where candles burned and smoking peat incense confirmed their appreciation for abundance and joy.

These ecological souls lived harmonically, each clan member tuned to Universal love.

Then, late one summer, the Christians sailed north, exploring the Dnieper River. The wafting aroma of roasting beef, onions, potatoes, and carrots lured them from the riverbank to the Healers' village, and the scent of baking bread led them even further into the catacombs, where young clan members ground grain and kept the oven fires burning.

The invaders claimed the caves in the name of Christianity and forced the men to build massive aboveground cathedrals and grind new cave entrances. Women were required to look after the children, tend the gardens, and prepare the meals. Men no longer played games with the children.

The Christians destroyed the hand-blown glass and carved idols, and forced the artisans to make swords, armor, and gates to keep out other invaders.

They burned profoundly insightful manuscripts written by wise women.

Filching parts of the Healers' spiritual wisdom as their own, the Christians used holy water and candlelight in their worshiping rituals and named just three spirit guides.

Worship of an almighty, judgmental, male God replaced simple gratitude.

Fear became all-powerful.

Patriarchy replaced natural harmonic essence.

Love between men and women was limited to procreation.

Self-love became unseemly.

The Healer's secrets were nearly lost.

Over time, many Healers were forced out of the city that would become Kiev. To survive, the Healers abandoned their enlightened energy. Some fled west to form a tribe later known as the Celts. Some fled south to become a clan of European Jews. Some stayed and conformed to the judgmental monotheistic religion while holding secret meetings beyond Christian view.

Thousands of wise and gifted evolutionary women, once focused on the potential of all humanity, were sentenced to death by hanging because they frightened the Christians and threatened their power.

One hundred generations of Healers crossed continents, sailed oceans, lived and died before the memory of their essence ignited like fire in the heart-memory of their descendants....

Yuri rested on his back with Morgan's head on his arm. Her back pressed against the side of his warm body as their indigo auras melted together. The love they felt for each other transcended time and space, and surpassed earthly, human desire.

Yuri had always known that his past life experiences influenced his current life on the planet but the details were unclear. He was certain that he had been divinely guided to Morgan's farm. This revelation proved beyond any doubt that he and Morgan had known each other many times before. "Do you remember those caves?" he asked, his voice soft and deep.

She stared, out of focus, into the eaves. "Yes.... Do you remember grinding the flour for bread?"

"Yes.... I remember pushing the big grinding stone. It must have been centuries old even then," he said. "I remember your dark eyelashes covered with fine white powder."

"Our little family was so young and happy when the invasion came. While I tended the fire under the bread ovens, you ground fresh flour. Even now, I smell the bread baking; I feel the heat of the oven on my face." She touched her own warm cheek. "Then they chased me through the catacombs... I can hear the slap of my bare feet on the warm earth...

I hear the baby's frightened cry and the toddler's scream. That day, they introduced fear for the first time."

"I couldn't find you. Did they take you away?" he said.

"They locked the baby and me in an empty cellar after taking all the meat. While I nursed our daughter, I watched ribbons of dusty light shimmer between cracks in the wooden door until… nightfall… total darkness. We must have died in there…. I hope our toddler survived. I heard his terrified screams as they carried him to the surface. He looked so much like you." Her eyes closed over sadness too deep for tears. "Where did they take you?"

"I remember grinding rock to make a new entrance to the cave below the church. The falling debris crushed me to death."

"The course of history changed that day," she said softly, "until then, we had no word for fear."

He rolled onto his side, pressing his chest against her back, the curve of his body matching hers. His arm drew her tight against him. Like petals of a water lily closing for the night, they fell sound asleep, exhausted from their journey across oceans, continents, and lifetimes.

The next day, they walked the tree farm for hours, quietly assimilating the memories. After dinner, Yuri went to his trailer to write while Morgan relaxed in her room, still weary from the previous night's intensity.

Suddenly, she turned off all the lights in the house and took a blanket into the dark yard by the gazebo. Lying on her back wrapped in the blanket, with Howard snuggled close, she watched the stars, no longer frightened by the dark.

chapter twenty-seven — olympic peninsula

When you are steadfast in your
abstention of thoughts of harm directed
toward others, all living creatures will
cease to feel enmity in your presence.

—Patanjali

"When was the last time you left this property for more than a few hours?"

"Ruth's funeral. Before that, the book show in Portland."

"If you don't have any bookings, let's drive over to the Olympic Peninsula tomorrow. You can get the neighbor girls to keep an eye on the animals."

"You mean overnight?"

"I'll sleep in the pickup, and you can sleep in the trailer."

Morgan laughed. "I forgot how portable your home is. Can we take Howard?"

"Of course. He'll love Ruby Beach. I'll reserve my favorite campsite at Kalaloch if that's okay."

"Wonderful."

While Morgan arranged for animal care, did her laundry, and packed some clothes, Yuri went to Central Market for supplies.

They pulled out of the driveway at precisely 8:00 a.m. the next morning.

"Can we stop at the post office in Sequim? We'll go right by—it'll only take a minute. I need to mail a present to Ruth's daughter, Sarah." Morgan held a small package containing a receiving blanket she knitted using white llama yarn dyed with natural yellow dye she had bought at The Artful Ewe in Port Gamble. "Her baby is due in June, and I want her to have this blanket ahead of time."

At the Kalaloch campground, Yuri pulled the trailer close to the bluff. He'd been there many times and knew exactly which campsite would offer the best view of the Pacific Ocean. They stood side by side breathing the calm, salty air with Howard sitting at Morgan's feet. The ocean reflected the sky as if one melted into the other with no visible horizon.

"What a gorgeous place! We couldn't be any closer to the ocean," *or each other,* she thought.

"Wait until dark—the stars are extraordinary. The vastness of the ocean seems to intensify their size and brightness."

They set up the trailer, then drove to Sol Duc Falls. Howard stayed in the truck—no dogs allowed.

"Too bad. I don't think he even knows he's a dog," Morgan laughed.

The dense forest felt damp and dark compared with the overgrown tree farm. The old growth stood heavy with wet moss hanging on every branch. They hiked alone on the trail; no other weekday visitor joined them. Yuri patiently waited while Morgan set up her tripod and photographed logs covered with mosses, lichens, and umbrella-like fungi. A mist rose around them as they listened to the roaring falls, swollen with melted snow. Connected with nature at every level—touch, sight, smell, sound, as well as energetically—they sat on damp mossy rocks with treasured silence between them.

After a while Yuri asked, "Have you ever seen the Hoh Rainforest?"

"I have, but I'd love to see it again. The trails are easy and not far from here."

When they returned to the truck, they found Howard asleep on the seat, apparently unaware they left him behind. They drove to the rainforest and walked the trails for an hour; then, while eating turkey sandwiches, drove north to Ruby Beach.

"Ruby Beach is my favorite place on the planet. Every time I visit, it looks different. Sometimes you have to climb over huge driftwood logs to get to the beach and other times the logs are gone and the beach is piled with flat, smooth rocks." As always, the haystack-like monoliths rose out of the sea, offering habitat for colonies of common murres and tufted puffins. Yuri pulled his binoculars out of his daypack to get a closer look.

"I've never seen a puffin," said Morgan. "They're so colorful and their beaks are so big, they look tropical."

Yuri and Morgan laughed as Howard chased a wave, then ran back up the packed sand as the waves chased him. His smile was contagious. The wet beach reflected his little white frame like a mirror.

"Don't worry, I brought extra towels to dry him after I hose him off. We won't track sand into your trailer."

"I'm not worried. He's having so much fun."

After a seafood dinner at the lodge, Yuri's treat, they spread a blanket on the dry sand at Kalaloch Beach and watched stars brighten the night sky. No artificial lights diluted the glow and only the sound of gentle waves disturbed the silence.

"Beautiful," Morgan whispered, as if her voice might interrupt the show. Howard burrowed between them.

"When I lived in Colorado, I drove the convertible into the mountains just to see the stars."

"Your mom let you drive her sports car?"

"That's the first car I drove. She got it the year I was born, so it was sixteen years old by the time I got my driver's license. Anyway, I'd put the top down and stargaze all night long. Sometimes Q-Zee came along. She told her mom she was spending the night with a friend. Actually, I think Mrs. Hanover knew we were together but my parents never did. Look!" He pointed at a shooting star. "The Lyrid meteor shower is this week."

"What's that?"

"Every April, the earth passes through the tail of a comet. Sometimes there can be over a hundred an hour. There's another… and another. They're at their peak tonight."

"If I understand what you said about the comet, the tail is there but we can't see it until the earth's atmosphere passes through it, like a layer of light waiting to be seen?"

"Excellent observation."

"Hey, how high does the tide come up on this beach?" Morgan asked. Just then, a salty wave flowed under their blanket.

"Geez! I forgot about the tide."

"Woohoo, that water's cold!" Morgan yelled as she grabbed Howard and ran up the bank toward the trailer, laughing. At the top she turned to him, "This is wonderful. I needed to get away from the farm for a while. Let's get up early and watch the sunrise from Hurricane Ridge."

Puffs of pink clouds reflected off the Strait of Juan de Fuca as they hiked Hurricane Ridge early the next morning. Morgan photographed deer that came close enough to touch. Signs everywhere reminded them, "Please, Don't Feed the Wild Animals."

"There's a wonderful trail down that way." Morgan pointed to the left of the visitor center. "I didn't know about it until I came here with Art Wolfe's photography workshop, long before I bought the farm. Let's leave Howard in the truck. He's exhausted from yesterday."

After enjoying the view at the end of the trail, they walked back up the ridge. Morgan asked Yuri, "When's your birthday?"

"December 22, 1972."

"So you'll be forty on December 22, 2012."

"Seems odd how fast forty is rolling around."

"Sagittarius or Capricorn?"

"Capricorn, but I haven't studied astrology much... yet," he said.

"Maybe we could—"

Yuri's arm flew sideways to stop Morgan. He bobbed his head toward the path they had walked less than an hour before. A black bear sat in the middle just twenty yards away with two small cubs climbing over her. The sow's heavy black coat glistened in the sun as she batted and played with her cubs, undisturbed by Yuri and Morgan's approach.

Morgan's heart pounded so loudly she worried the bear could hear it. She tried not to breathe. Finally, the mother bear looked up. Morgan saw the bear's white teeth as the red tongue licked around her black muzzle. Her huge claws flicked gravel as the sow took three slow steps towards them. Then she turned to amble into the underbrush, the chubby cubs rolling over each other as they disappeared behind her.

Yuri and Morgan remained still, almost breathless, for several minutes more. Morgan might have remained motionless if Yuri hadn't urged her on.

"I'm sure it's safe to pass. She knows we mean no harm."

Morgan stood frozen with gratitude, not fear. Tears dripped from her chin. "Yuri, I heard you talk to her. And she spoke to you."

Tears welled in Yuri's eyes too. "Incredible, isn't it? I'm glad you could hear it."

Yuri and the bear had used an ancient form of communication, each understanding the other, each respecting the other.

"I'm aware of something more. I didn't have the ability to speak, so I became invisible to her. I blended with the trees with nothing to hide. She saw only you, not me." Morgan paused then said, "I think I first learned to do that when Doc started abusing my brother. He never hit me."

"Like the shamans. Shape-shifting," he said.

Morgan nodded and felt as if a part of her floated above the ground as they started to walk towards the parking area.

"You're probably right, she heard me and didn't see you. She knew her cubs weren't in danger. One thing for sure, she didn't smell very good."

Their laughter helped Morgan relax and ground herself again. When they joined Howard in the truck, he wildly sniffed the air around them.

"I'm sure glad we left you here," Morgan said as she rubbed Howard's ears.

While Yuri backed the trailer into the clearing, Morgan called to thank the neighbors. Then she walked to the barn, filled the llama's bin with hay and sat on the hayloft stairs. The llamas stood nearby, eating, apparently ignoring her.

I wonder if I'll ever be able to communicate with animals the way Yuri does, she thought.

Lars and Luna both curled their long necks to listen to her thoughts.

chapter twenty-eight —
yuri leaves

*"Don't grieve. Anything you lose
comes round in another form."*

—Rumi

Yuri entered the kitchen as if dragging lead boots. His red pickup and the Airstream trailer waited in the driveway like a two-car train, ready for his trip to California.

"All set?" Morgan said softly.

"Guess so."

"I'll miss you," she said, reaching for a hug.

"And I'll miss you." Yuri hugged her back, but harder. "Let's go for a walk in the tree farm before I go."

The sun would soon slide behind the Olympic Mountains. Although he had procrastinated all day, he still planned to drive to a familiar campground near Salem, Oregon.

Beams of amber sunlight turned cobwebs to golden threads connecting rows of naturally shaped fir and spruce, Christmas trees too mature to harvest. Wet grass rustled underfoot as Howard smelled every tuft. They walked silently for a few minutes.

"I hope you know how much I appreciate your help," she said.

"This place provided the solitude I needed to work on my next book. You opened your house and your heart to me." Despite his efforts, a tear trickled down his cheek.

"I learned so much from you. There aren't any accidents when it comes to this stuff." A tremble rose in her voice.

Further into the forest, under huge cedar branches, they discussed reincarnation and multiple levels of time and space.

"Time is an illusion," he said. "We humans need to measure time to maintain our linear lives, but I think everything happens at the same time, like channels on the TV. The mystical universe is measured in levels of awareness rather than minutes. The soul incarnates to accomplish something. You could even meet your own soul in another human body."

The path turned back toward an open area where Mr. Wakefield and his grandson had planted rows of Noble Fir seedlings, Christmas trees of the future. They walked in silence, as if their conversation required the protection of tall trees. Finally, Morgan asked, "You mean a soul could be on earth more than once—simultaneously?"

"It could. If we met in human form, we wouldn't recognize ourselves," he said.

Morgan contemplated the possibility of dual existence on earth and life without time.

"Everything is connected, what is and what could be. If humans understood how our lives are linked, the impact could be powerful." Yuri's voice held a deep timbre. He didn't sound like himself.

"What about gender? Do we always come back—or exist simultaneously—as the same sex?" she asked.

"Gender is irrelevant to the spirit world. One incarnation could be as a male, another as a female. It depends on what your spirit needs to learn. We incarnate to accomplish goals or gain experience—for ourselves or to help others." Then he asked, "Do you ever think about the purpose of *your* life?"

"I never used to. I couldn't see the difference between my Self and my job. We talked about that before. Now I know it's all about love." Big tears rolled down her cheeks. "Yuri, I never knew how love felt until I met you. I thought love was a fairytale, a movie theme."

Green heart-light swirled between them as they walked.

Moving out of the trees, marginally within time and space, she picked up a twig covered with mosses and lichens. She held it gently, lightly brushing her palm over the soft, damp surface, enjoying its faint, colorful glow and musty fragrance. "How many people would bother to notice this micro rain- forest?" To her the twig represented the layers of consciousness unnoticed by most of the human race.

"Not many," Yuri agreed, aware of her deeper meaning.

"How much goes unnoticed by all of us, even you and me. The world could be full of comet dust, but we can't see until we run through it. If we're unaware, do we see reality? Do we miss the level of consciousness you're talking about? What's here, on the planet that humans can't see, or won't see, because it's unfamiliar?"

"Do you remember when you served that fruit jelly... what was it?"

"*Membrillo*," Morgan said, smiling at the memory of Yuri devouring the leftover stuffed French toast. "I used the neighbor's quince."

"I'd never heard of quince. Then I passed a big display at Central Market. A couple of days later, I saw an article about the history of the quince tree. Once I'd been introduced to it, quince seemed to be everywhere. Of course, quince had been there all along. My awareness changed. The same is true with metaphysical phenomena, like the night your father visited your office. Things like that happen all the time. However, for unaware humans, that part of reality is invisible. As you said at the time, if I hadn't been there to help, you would have missed his visit. He floated beyond your understanding."

They stood quietly, bathed in fuchsia-tinted light reflected by the clouds after sunset.

As they walked out of the underbrush, a trained and sensitive observer would have noticed their intermingled auras radiating indigo with bright golden streaks.

They crossed the road and quietly pulled tall grass to feed the llamas. Yuri stepped to the fence and Lars moved forward to meet him, allowing Yuri to rub his long neck.

"I'm going to miss you, Lars."

Lars rested his chin on Yuri's shoulder.

Yuri didn't want to leave and Morgan didn't want him to go. Morgan had never felt so close to another human being. Through Yuri, she'd learned that a man and a woman could love each other and enjoy spiritual intimacy far beyond the need or desire for a physical relationship.

As they came through the back door, Morgan said, "Why don't you get a good night's rest, and leave in the morning. Traffic won't be bad on Sunday. The guest room in the back is ready."

"That's a good idea," he said. "I'm feeling sort of weird. Are you sure you don't mind re-setting that room?"

"Of course not, but thanks for asking. Let's sit by the fire in the living room. You want a beer or a glass of wine?"

"Not tonight," he said. "But tea would be nice."

As Morgan brewed two cups of herbal tea, she glanced at the clock on the microwave. Returning to the living room, she handed Yuri a red mug, switched on the gas fireplace, then sat in the chair across from him, the buff leather squeaking as she settled in. "Yuri, how long does it usually take us to walk the tree farm?"

"About an hour—more or less. We walked slowly tonight, so probably longer. Why?"

"According to the clock, we were gone only ten minutes. How did we do that?"

"No wonder I feel so weird. We went on a trip together."

"What do you mean, *trip*?"

"Have you ever heard of *astral projection*[14]?"

"Sure. I think I've even done it—maybe in dreams—but I've never heard of *astral projection* with another person."

"Why not? I felt close to you out there. Time and space seemed irrelevant. Didn't you sense that?"

"Yeah… but… ten minutes?"

"Apparently," he shrugged, his blue eyes twinkling.

She noticed he looked happy, relaxed, calm. Morgan felt the same stillness.

---

14   **astral projection** *or astral travel an interpretation of out-of-body experience that assumes the existence of an astral body, capable of traveling outside of the physical body. Astral projection or travel denotes the astral body leaving the physical body to travel in the astral plane.*

"I'm sure we'll do it again sometime," he said. "Maybe we can meet on the astral plane while I'm in California."

"Are you saying that we could travel like that intentionally?"

"Why not? By now you know all we need to do is ask," he said.

At four the next morning, Yuri drove under the ancient fir and turned south, avoiding the last goodbye.

Morgan's youthful curiosity and endless enthusiasm fascinated him. During his five-month stay on her farm, he watched her intuitive and clairvoyant gifts emerge while her fear and self-doubt subsided. Morgan had helped him as well. They amplified each other's energy, a rare gift in itself. She had confidence in him and allowed his help in all areas of her life. Morgan appreciated everything he did for her, both his earthly skills and his spiritual and intuitive skills—the abilities that made him who he was, the part of him his parents had denied.

He stopped for breakfast at a diner near the Columbia River in Oregon. After ordering, he called Morgan from his cell phone.

"Sorry I left without saying goodbye."

"It was easier that way."

"You can call me whenever you want; I've always got my cell phone with me. If I don't answer, I'll return your call as soon as I can."

"What am I going to have for dinner? I got used to having meals cooked for me," she tried to joke.

"You managed to eat before I got there."

"I had more fun eating meals with you...."

"My breakfast is ready. Remember, we don't need to sit by the fire every night to stay close."

"Yes, I know... enjoy your breakfast and drive safe."

"We'll talk soon," he said.

She hung up the phone, robotically stepped into her Uggs, and dragged herself across the road to the tree farm. Howard walked slowly beside her, his tail dragging on the gravel.

chapter twenty-nine — the chick

Your task is not to seek for love, but
merely to seek and find all the barriers
within yourself that you have built
against it.

—Rumi

As Morgan and Howard returned from their walk, she heard a peeping sound. Walking across the pasture, the sound grew louder. In the top nesting box, she found a tiny Black Silky chick. When she picked it up, the chick burrowed into her sleeve and quieted.

With her free hand, she maneuvered a heat lamp out of the barn. In the garage she found a box, went back to the barn to fill it with straw bedding, then up to the house, all the while keeping the chick warm in her sleeve.

Howard patiently watched Morgan prepare the nest in her bathroom. She needed both hands to rig the heat lamp, so she put the chick on the floor, and it began peeping. The chick quieted again when it found Howard's warm belly and snuggled as if the dog were a big white hen.

Howard smiled up at Morgan.

"Howard, you are the gentlest dog ever."

The next day she put the little chick on the floor and it followed her to the kitchen. For several days, she did very little without the black two-footed fluff-ball close behind. The chick sat on Howard's back as Morgan pulled a few weeds around the peonies and euphorbia, then it followed her back to the house, flapping its fuzzy wings to keep up. One day, as little feathers replaced down, she left it in the duck's coop while she fed the llamas, then ran into the house to answer the phone. After booking a guest for the coming weekend, she returned to the coop. When she started to fill the water trough, there floated the dead chick.

Morgan always suffered an out-of-proportion sense of vulnerability and loss when the eagles took her ducks and chickens. This loss felt far worse. The tiny creature depended on her for food, shelter, and safety, and she had failed as its mother hen.

She buried the chick under the dogwood tree and marked the diminutive grave with a huge green rock she rolled up from the pond.

In mid-afternoon, the temperature hovered near seventy, but she took a shower, put on her red polar fleece bathrobe, switched on the fireplace, and lit candles. Sarajane Williams's *Harp Music for Healing* played on the small stereo as she stared into the flames, glad there were no bookings.

As usual, Howard rested his chin on her knee. She sat quietly, stroking his fur and watching the orange flames dance. Howard jumped down and ran out of the room. She heard him digging in his basket of toys. He returned with his teddy bear. He jumped back onto the sofa, put his teddy in her lap, then snuggled close again, just as he had done for Biz after Ruth died.

Did Howard know the chick had drowned? Did he know that summer bookings weren't covering winter expenses? Did he understand how much she missed Yuri? For certain, he felt her pain and tried to comfort her.

They sat for hours watching the fire. The room grew overheated, but she couldn't move. She ignored the ringing phone. It rang again and again, and finally she got up.

"Hello?" she answered, forgetting her usual customer service script.

"Are you okay?" asked Yuri. "I felt a shift earlier today. I couldn't call until now."

"You felt a shift? All the way from Tahoe?"

"That shouldn't surprise you. Did something happen?"

"The day you left, a little Silky chick hatched."

"I thought you gathered all the eggs every day."

"Well, apparently for twenty-eight days, little Betty Bantam tucked the egg under her wing, but she abandoned the hatchling."

"You still haven't answered my question."

"The poor little thing imprinted on me, followed me everywhere. I had to be careful not to step on it. Well... this afternoon... it drowned."

"You've lost chickens before. Why is this one different?"

"I don't know.... I guess my emotions are raw since you left.... Worrying that I won't be able to cover winter expenses doesn't help either." Words caught in her chest.

"Hello? Morgan? Are you there?"

"Sorry, yes, sorry, I'm here. I miss you Yuri. I miss you. I've realized how... how much I love you."

"I love you too."

"I know you love me," she said, and for the first time in her life, she meant it. "I told you about seeing the pillars of light in the corner of my bedroom that night and the intense love I felt while they were there. That made sense to me. It felt real and right. Now I know that it's possible for me to feel loved by a man, a real human man, and I know it's not because he wants to have sex with me. This love makes the other kind seem crass."

"Yes," he said softly, "I'm glad you're all right. I knew I needed to talk with you as soon as I could... the vibration felt intense. I'd like to talk more about this, but I need a shower and food. I've been working all day, and I'm pretty ripe. Can I call you later tonight?"

"Of course, I'm fine. Really, I'm fine."

Morgan turned off the fireplace and opened the windows as sparkling twilight illuminated the snowcapped mountains. She picked up Howard and walked up the stairs to her room. He uncharacteristically licked her cheek—maybe her face tasted salty from her tears or maybe he loved her too.

A little after eleven, as she sat on the bed knitting, the phone rang.

"Feeling better?" he said.

"I guess so. I had to process the feelings. It took a while."

"Did you learn anything?"

Morgan hesitated and he listened to her silence.

"You taught me about love," she said.

"You taught yourself."

"Maybe that's true. You led me, or opened the door, or took away the barriers—regardless of the metaphor, I needed help to find love and you materialized."

"I'll accept that," he said.

"It's not the love I miss—that's still here—like the love a flower feels for the rain, or the ocean feels for the shore, or a tree feels for the land. I wish our language had more words for the concept of love. Now that I know that love is inside me and I'm not dependent on another human, love is everywhere, every minute, as long as I slow down and find quiet.... It's all about silence." She took a deep breath. "The chick seemed happy being a baby chick—growing, eating, sleeping. I projected love onto it and love back from it. Maybe its purpose on the planet was to remind me that love is everywhere." Again she paused. "I learned something more..."

"Take your time. This isn't a race."

Her hands felt wet with his tears, as if she held his face in her palms.

"I learned that a soul might come to the planet just to help another soul do something important, learn something key, be something better. We think that a human lifetime of eighty or a hundred years is a long time. But in the journey of a soul, it's less than a nanosecond. Our story, the story of Yuri and Morgan, is a story of many lifetimes, I'm certain, but that's not what I'm talking about. That's different from this...." Morgan's voice trailed off and Yuri sensed her struggling for the right words. "You're doing great. I feel your energy, I hear the music, it's beautiful. You don't need to rush; take your time."

"I'm wondering… if my father came to the planet—as a human, I mean—if he came to the planet to help me in what appeared to be a negative way, maybe it's the only way I—my soul—could truly experience the absence of real love. Now it seems so simple, not difficult at all. Love comes from inside. You must learn to love yourself before you can love another. My father embodied the opposite; it appeared that he loved no one, especially himself. All my life, I tried to prove that his anger and sadness had nothing to do with me. Then I learned to love you...

and to allow you to love me... because I learned to love my Self. Accept my Self. Like Doc said that night—he didn't know me. As a human, he couldn't SEE me like you do.... Maybe his soul sacrificed a turn on the planet to help me find the wisdom of love... and so did that baby chick."

"That's a big lesson to learn from a tiny creature," he said.

chapter thirty — the birth

Tell me, what is it you plan to do with
your one wild and precious life?
—Mary Oliver

"Hi, Morgan," said Sarah, Ruth's daughter.

"Sarah! Hi! How are you?"

"Considering how big I'm getting, I'm doing great. The reason I'm calling…."

Sarah inherited the best of her Aunt Biz *and* her mother. A powerful attorney, she had a head for business and a heart for love. She understood her mother's metaphysical beliefs. Morgan could hear that Sarah was crying. "Sarah, what is it?"

Sarah swallowed her grief. "We're planning a home birth. Mom planned to be here with us but… now… well…."

Morgan stood silent, allowing Sarah to catch her breath.

"We were wondering if you could be here instead. You've been like an aunt to me… and… I know you understand, better than anyone, that Mom will be with us in her own way…."

"Oh, Sarah, I'd be honored." Morgan and Sarah had enjoyed a special bond since the moment they met when Sarah was about ten. Even as a little girl, Sarah had her mother's exceptional understanding of the world. When Morgan first met Ruth, their daughters were in elementary school. Occasionally Ruth and Morgan would take their daughters to the zoo or the aquarium. Every Christmas, they saw the Nutcracker Ballet together and enjoyed a fancy dinner afterwards. Occasionally Biz came along on their outings, but she lacked the patience required to deal with children. Morgan's friendship with Biz spun around their business lives while her friendship with Ruth was family-centered.

"I'll keep you posted. Hopefully you can catch a ferry and be here in time if we call you when I go into labor. Our midwife, Hazel, will be with us, of course."

"Sarah, I can't wait! I'll be there if I have to swim!"

Morgan knew the inn would be booked. *Somehow, I'll make it work.*

On the day Sarah went into labor, Morgan had a *whole house booking*, one family occupied the entire inn. Henri and Jacqueline had been there twice before, and this time they brought his family, visiting from France. She felt comfortable leaving them to enjoy their time together. She knew that her decision to offer whole-house bookings was no accident, *it was part of the cosmic plan*, she thought.

She arranged for the neighbor girls to feed the animals and took Howard with her. When she arrived at Jim and Sarah's house, she left Howard sleeping in the truck and hurried up the walk. Hazel, the midwife, met her at the door.

"You must be Morgan."

"Hello, Hazel. I hope I'm not too late."

"You made it. Sarah worried about you, but I think that might have kept her mind occupied. She misses her mother. She and Jim are in the bedroom upstairs. Everything is going according to plan. I want you to know, though, if I thought there was the slightest possibility that she would have a problem with this birth, I'd recommend the hospital."

"I'm glad to hear that. I guess women have been having babies at home for centuries. Still, it's a little unsettling."

"She'll do just fine."

After washing her hands, Morgan followed Hazel upstairs. They paused outside the bedroom door as Jim coached Sarah through a contraction.

"Heee, heee, heee… that's it, you're doing great. We're almost there."

Sarah sat halfway up, her back supported by pillows. Her big belly rose between her bent legs covered with a white sheet.

Morgan followed Hazel into the room with the glasses riding low on the bridge of her nose.

"Hi, Morgan." Sarah reached for a hug. "I'm so glad you made it."

"Hi, sweetheart. You doin' okay?"

"Yes, but… contractions aren't any fun."

"They'll be all over before you know it, and it'll be so, so worth it." Morgan patted the about-to-be-daddy on the back, "Congratulations, Jim."

Hazel walked to the foot of the bed.

"Let's take a peek," she said as she lifted the sheet. "Looks like you're fully dilated. Morgan got here just in time."

Jim and Hazel helped Sarah scoot closer to the foot of the bed as they had planned. Morgan tried to make herself useful by fluffing pillows. Hazel tucked the sheet above the taut belly and glanced at Jim and Sarah with a kind, reassuring smile.

"It's time to birth this baby. Jim, you sit behind Sarah, as you practiced, and help her remember to breathe between contractions. Sarah, when the next one comes, wait until I tell you, then push." Hazel took her place on a little stool at the foot of the bed and pulled on fresh gloves.

"I love you," Jim said softly in Sarah's ear as tears streamed down his face, and their eyes embraced. Then he sat on the bed behind her.

She gripped his arm and smiled, then squealed, "Woo-ah, here comes a big one."

Hazel said, "That's it, now PUSH!"

A few minutes later, as the baby girl came into the light, a vacuum pulled air from the small space. Morgan lost her breath. A vague misty glow slowly materialized. Then, even though the windows and doors were closed, a light breeze swirled the scent of freshness.

It all happened so fast. Hazel looked up at Jim. Without a word, he stepped to the foot of the bed. Towering over Hazel, who still sat on her little stool, he accepted the surgical scissors and cut the umbilical cord as Hazel indicated. Luminosity of joy, expectation, and awe permeated the air. The wet, naked baby wailed her first wail as Morgan watched the tiny body absorb the steamy glow that had appeared only moments before.

Theologians and other spiritual leaders disagree on the exact moment a soul and a baby find each other, but with the help of the glasses, Morgan witnessed the union of body and soul.

Hazel must have seen this many times, Morgan thought.

Hazel looked Morgan in the eye and gave her a knowing nod, then nimbly swaddled the baby.

"I'd say about six pounds," Hazel proclaimed. "What's her name?"

Simultaneously, Sarah and Jim answered, "Ruth."

"Perfect…." Morgan said quietly. Little Ruthie would grow up without her grandmother, but she would have her name.

Hazel put the baby into the arms of her emotional new daddy. Jim unbuttoned his shirt so Ruthie's cheek could rest on his bare skin. Then, when Sarah was ready, he unwrapped the baby, put her on her mother's exposed chest, and covered them both with the llama fiber blanket Morgan had mailed in April.

Sarah glowed. "Here I am, skin to skin with my newborn daughter, and just minutes ago an unknown infant waited inside me. It's overwhelming." Sarah touched her baby's cheek. "Thanks for being here, Morgan."

"I'm the grateful one," said Morgan. "I'm glad I made it in time, and I didn't have to swim!" She didn't need to mention how much they all missed Ruth, but Morgan knew Ruth lingered nearby, and Sarah knew as well. "I wonder what little Ruthie's plans are now that she's got birth out of the way."

They all laughed and cried together, even Hazel.

"You want to hold her?" Sarah asked.

"I'd love to!"

Hazel quickly re-swaddled the baby with expert precision and placed the bundle in the bend of Morgan's arm.

"Hi, Ruthie," said Morgan through the glasses as she gently touched the baby's cheek with the back of her hand. "You can call me *Auntie Mo….*" She glanced up at Sarah, beaming back at her.

Calm permeated the air. The infant opened her eyes and peered deep into Morgan's soul. Morgan could see the indigo light around the baby. She said quietly, "Ruthie, I'm grateful to meet you and I promise I'll do anything I can to help you learn and grow, always, just like your grandmother and namesake…." Morgan almost said *if she were here* but then, through the glasses, she saw Ruth, bending close, kissing the baby's cheek. *Congratulations, Grandma.*

The corners of the baby's tiny mouth turned up as if smiling at the thought of getting to know them. Ruthie wiggled inside the soft yellow blanket, and Morgan felt a little personality emerging as an air of wisdom beyond her minutes of life swirled around them.

chapter thirty-one —
morgan hill's retreat

So that for the first time
you can walk away from that place,
Reunited with your banished heart,
now healed and freed,
And feel the clear, free air bless your new face.

—John O'Donohue,
To Bless the Space Between Us

FROM MID-JUNE TO MID-SEPTEMBER, every year Morgan prepared breakfast ninety days in a row, although sadly, not always for a full house. Few guests appreciated the expense or effort required to serve a gourmet meal. She learned to serve more cost-effective breakfasts but in the end, it didn't matter. Summer bookings could not sustain year-round expenses, and with the failing real estate market, the mortgage outweighed the property value. Meanwhile, the bank froze the equity line-of-credit she used to make ends meet during the off-season.

After five seasons as an inn keeper, Morgan closed the B&B and put the farm up for sale. She remembered what Yuri had said: "It's all about the attitude. Remember, you get what you think you'll get."

She walked the labyrinth with the intention of selling the property for what she had paid for it. And with intention, she visualized the quiet cottage where she would live in solitude without judgment and continue on the path of awareness.

Even after closing the B&B, Morgan robotically answered the phone, "Morgan Hill Retreat. This is Morgan. How can I help you?"

"Hi Morgan, Lyn here. I thought you closed the B&B," said Lyn, the owner of Dauntless Books in Port Gamble.

"Hi, Lyn. I did. Old habits are difficult to break, I guess. What's up?"

"What are your plans? Are you going to stay in the area?"

"That's the plan, if I can find a little cottage on the beach. I want to write another book."

"I hoped you'd say that. I need to rent the property my parents built as a summer place. They lived there year-round for the last 10 years, until they moved to the Martha and Mary Retirement Home a few months ago. I thought you might want to rent it."

"Tell me about it." Manifesting what she wanted had become part of her life. She felt reverence and gratitude but not surprise.

"It's a cozy little cottage—only eight hundred square feet, the perfect writer's retreat. It has two bedrooms, a propane furnace, and a big fireplace, with lots of wood you're welcome to burn. Dad loved gardening so the property is spectacular, with old rhodies, azaleas, and perennials. There's a gnarled old quince tree Dad planted when they first bought the property. It started blooming this week. If you like to make quince jam, you'll have all the fruit you need."

Morgan smiled, remembering the membrillo Yuri liked so much.

"You can see Mt. Baker from the living room, and there are steps down to the beach. It's not far from my store. I need the income to pay for taxes, maintenance, and the gardener, but mostly I just want someone living there who will care for it as their home."

"I'd love to see it. How's tomorrow after you close?"

"Great. Meet me at the store and we'll walk over on the beach."

Lyn's parents purchased the three acres of land on Teekalet Bluff after World War II. When Lyn and her brother were children, her mother pitched a tent on the property and they camped every summer until they built the cottage. Lyn's father worked in Seattle during the week and spent the weekends with the family—fishing, beachcombing, and tinkering in the garden.

As Lyn and Morgan walked up the steps from the beach, Morgan gasped, "What a beautiful cottage!" Huge windows flanked the living room. From the porch, Morgan could see through the living room to the forest on the other side. At one end of the living room, a beach rock fireplace stood floor to ceiling. On the other end, the kitchen was open, with a big island and stools. The appliances were like new, the walls freshly painted, and the hardwood floors perfect for the rugs Morgan had made from llama fiber. The big claw-footed tub invited relaxation next to a private courtyard filled with rhododendron in full bloom. Every room except for the bathroom and little bedroom in the back had sweeping northern views of Hood Canal, with the Olympic Mountains to the west and Mount Baker to the northeast.

"This is gorgeous! Are you sure $800 a month is enough?" Morgan asked in spite of herself. "It's perfect, just what I hoped to find. I can't ask you to keep it open for me, but I'd love to live here if everything works out with the sale of the farm."

The next day, the realtor brought Morgan an offer. "It's full price. I've seen nothing like it in this market. AND they want to keep the animals!"

Thanks, Yuri. It's all about attitude.

Without the slightest concern that the deal might not go through, Morgan paid Lyn a security deposit plus first and last months' rent, then called *Two Men and a Truck* to schedule the move.

Hoping to simplify her life and jettison anything that wouldn't fit into the cottage, she made lists: what to give her daughter, what to take to the cottage, what to sell and for how much. On Sunday, her daughter, Maggie and her husband came with a truck to gather the things Morgan set aside for them.

On Monday, the movers hauled the bed from the Sunflower Suite, a dresser that Morgan inherited from her grandparents, a sofa, lamps and other furniture as well as carefully packed boxes. Then Morgan and her friends organized the estate sale.

On Tuesday and Wednesday before the advertised weekend sale, her neighbors and friends gathered to help sort, price and tag. They filled one guest room with Christmas decorations and another with linens, pillows and spa bathrobes. They used another guest room to display watercolor paints, pastels, and other art supplies as well as Morgan's collection of film cameras. Tables in the living room held dishes, glassware, pots and pans, serving trays, small appliances and nick-nacks.

She kept telling herself, *It's just stuff. I'll never need any of it again.* However, her feelings changed when bargain hunters and antique dealers mobbed the farm on Saturday morning. With the glasses on her nose, she and her friends tended to the parade of strangers marching off with her lifelong collection of treasures from all over the world.

"Will you take a dollar for this teapot?"

"The one I used to serve special guests when I lived in Hong Kong?" she said.

On Sundays, if she wasn't working, Morgan took long walks through the humid streets of Hong Kong, ducking in and out of dark, dusty shops. Ice House Street, in the Central District, was lined with antique shops filled with remarkably low-priced treasures that were hundreds of years old. The merchant wrapped the blue and white teapot with layers Chinese newsprint and Morgan carried it all the way back to her flat in Wan Chai.

"Will you take five dollars for this carved horse head?"

"The one I bought on Laxmie Road in Pune, India?" said Morgan.

While living in a flat on Koregaon Park Road in Pune, India, just south of the Mula-Mutha River, Morgan went to the Laxmie market for groceries every Saturday at 4:00 p.m. Her driver, uncomfortable with a woman shopping alone, followed her around the market. With hand gestures and head shaking, he offered his advice on ripe mangos and fresh vegetables. He spoke no English.

He followed her into a dark smelly shop where she found old wood carvings covered with decades filth. She paid 80 rupees (about $2.00) for an intricately carved, life-size horse head. The driver carried the carving to the car, no doubt curious about her need for such an old, dirty piece of wood. Using dish soap and a scrub brush, she cleaned it and left it on the terrace in the hot sun. Once dry, she realized the carving was even more beautiful than she'd hoped.

"How much for this wooden bucket?"

"The one I bought in Xixia, China?" she said.

Her friends planned a trip to Xixia, China. Sharon and Mel had never been out of the US and asked Morgan to join them. They met in San Francisco for the flight to Hong Kong, flew to Shanghai, then boarded a train to Xixia, stopping for overnight stays in villages along the way. When they got to the strangely American hotel in Xixia that Mel had booked on line, the porter insisted on caring Morgan's camera along with her luggage. While they waited on the elevator, he dropped the camera on the cement floor.

In her room, Sharon, Mel, and Morgan hovered over the camera like doctors in an operating room. Eventually they removed the bent lens cap and the shattered UV filter. Relieved, Morgan continued to take photos during the trip. Her favorite was of a little girl with a chin-length bob wearing a red jacket and nuzzling a yellow baby chick.

"What's this thing?" a child asked, holding up what might have been a wooden rattle, with a delicately carved cylinder of wood on a wooden handle.

She took it from the boy and held it with two hands. "This is a prayer wheel from Nepal. The Nepalese believe that spinning it will send prayers to the heavens." Morgan demonstrated.

"I'll give you a dollar," said the mother.

Morgan rolled it in her palms. She brought the carving to her face and smelled the wood. Memories of her trip to Nepal flooded back.

The pungent scent of incense lured Morgan into a monastery in Kathmandu. The monks wore ruby-red robes. Their shaved heads bobbed in perfect rows. The drone of their chanting voices awoke something inside her, launching chills up her spine and driving tears of gratitude down her cheeks.

Like other tourists, she spun the huge cylindrical prayer wheels that were carved from dark wood but worn pale where centuries of hopeful hands had turned them, spinning prayers to the heavens.

In a little shop next to the temple, a small brown-skinned little boy with a beautiful white smile sold small wooden replicas. Morgan made a ceremony of selecting the perfect prayer wheel and bargained with the child, as expected. Then, with both hands, she gave him a five-dollar bill, the equivalent of 225 in rupees. "This is for you," she said.

The boy quickly found a hinged cloisonné box shaped like a tiny trunk, big enough to hold four aspirin, and presented it to Morgan with both hands and a big grin. "This gift you," he said in his best English.

It was the first time she'd noticed that inanimate objects could be imbued with energy. Morgan sat on a stone wall, clutching the little box in one hand and the prayer wheel in the other, as if they told a story she had yet to understand.

She watched the throng of locals walk the dusty path below. Clouds of bright magenta, golden-yellow, and emerald-green fabrics floated around the women like prayer flags. They carried supplies on their heads; baskets filled with tangled yard-long beans, spikey green jackfruit, smooth yellow mangos, and prickly red lychee. One woman balanced a fax machine.

"Sorry. No, I need to keep this." She wrapped the prayer wheel in newspaper and locked it in the cab of the pickup where Howard waited with his usual tolerance.

One thoughtless woman asked, "Was it your mother who died?"

Morgan stared at the women without expression, then said, "No, it was me."

The woman watched with an open mouth as Morgan walked out of the house.

She liberated Howard from the truck, then told the friend who guarded the cash box, "I'll be back in a few minutes, Howard needs to do his thing." Leading Howard on a leash, his short legs spinning to keep up, she walked stiffly to the cold fire pit. She sat on the ground where her Adirondack chair once stood, and she sobbed.

After Fishline Charity had picked up the last unsold items, Morgan cleaned every inch of the house as if guests' might see that dust had accumulated behind furniture. Late in the day, stiff and tired, she walked slowly through the pristine, empty house. Howard looked up at her, his tail hanging low. Rubbing his soft white fur, she carried him up the stairs and stood at the railing, looking down into the empty living room. Suddenly remembering the trunk, she pulled the red handle, unfolding the stairs, and entered the dim attic with Howard under her arm.

She reached for the glasses tucked in her hair, but the glasses were gone.

Descending the stairs in one leap, she retraced her steps through the empty house. She searched the kitchen, looked around the garage, inspected the barn, and combed every inch of the truck. Then she remembered leaning over to pack dishes for a bargain hunter.

They must have fallen into that box, she thought.

Certain that the glasses were nowhere on the property, she returned to the empty house. Each step echoed across the naked wood floor and sage-green walls....

She remembered the dancing orbs and peculiar music.... She remembered Ruth and Sammy on the dewy grass under the stars.... She remembered the light and scent of freshness at the moment of Ruthie's birth.... *How can I go back to the life I knew before the glasses?*

She climbed back to the dim attic. Fatigue and sadness overwhelmed her. She spread the quilt as if planning a picnic, knelt on the floor and rolled onto her side. Her eyes grew heavy, as clouds reflected the rosy twilight.

"Don' allow dah sadness, dear heart," said the voice of Áine Mary Morgan. *"My darlin' girl, you won' be needin' my glasses to see whawt ya need ta see. In my day, folks not understandin' forced us awt a Ireland 'cause our gifts frightened 'em. Yer time's better nahw. Ya won' be cast awt for believin' in dah spirits or seein' dah colours 'r sharin' whah ya see, an' knaw, an' feel. My glasses taught ya how ta see. Don' ya worry, darlin' girl, ya don' need 'em any longer."*

Morgan awoke after midnight with the attic's peculiar light around her. She saw the colorful orbs dancing as swans in the rafters, just as the day she found the glasses. She heard the music of their harp-like voices.

Now, even stronger than the day she found the glasses, universal love permeated the air and saturated her heart. She took the clàrsach from the trunk and hugged it to her in the dark, afraid that without the glasses, her fingers couldn't play. Her fingertips brushed something on the base of the harp and she turned it over. Walking to the window for better light, she read:

For my beloved wife Suzanne Margaret

Sean Michael Morgan, 1896

Port Gamble, Washington

Sean Michael Morgan was Áine Mary Morgan's grandson, thought Morgan. She played a soft melody, then, overwhelmed with the events of the past few weeks, and warmed by this discovery, she fell asleep wrapped in the quilt, Howard by her side.

At daybreak, Morgan and Howard walked the tree farm. They passed Mr. Wakefield climbing onto his tractor, ready to cultivate between the rows of Christmas tree seedlings.

"Mornin'," he said. "You sleep all alone in that empty house last night?"

"One last time." She smiled up at him, shading her eyes from the morning sun, knowing that she had been less alone than any time in her life. She would never feel alone again. "I almost forgot my old trunk in the attic. Can you help me carry it out to the truck?"

"Be happy ta help," he said as he climbed down from the tractor.

"Mr. Wakefield, how long have you owned the tree farm?" she asked as they walked across the road.

"My father bought this here hundred acres from an Irishman named Sean Morgan in the twenties, 'bout the time I was born. The family owned thousands a acres, called it Sawdust Hill. Put cattle on some of it. Made his money sellin' timber and workin' over at the lumber mill in

Port Gamble. Story is, after he died, the family had trouble payin' taxes so they sold it off piece by piece."

"So Sean Morgan owned my property too?"

"Sure did. The granddaughter, Margaret Morgan married Frank Braun. They took over the farmin' in the forties. He was a grumpy ol'codger. Never seemed to like cattle much, or anything else for that matter, built that house you been livin' in. When Frank died, they sold everything 'cept your five acres. Then after Ol' Lady Braun died, and the daughter sold it ta you." Mr. Wakefield's voice echoed through the empty house as they entered through the back door. "Now where's that there trunk at?"

Morgan and Mr. Wakefield carried the trunk down the steps and out the back door to the truck bed.

"It's been real nice bein' yer neighbor. Hope we run inta each other from time ta time."

"Me too, Mr. Wakefield. Thanks for the help. Say good-bye to your grandson for me."

"Will do. Bye now."

They shook hands and Morgan watched him slowly walk down the driveway under the big fir. He was a lot older than she'd thought. As she started to close the gate of the pickup, something caught her eye. Small letters tooled in the leather on the back of the trunk:

S.D.L. ~ 1838.

She'd never noticed the inscription.

Sean David Lowery had crafted the trunk for his sister's sixteenth birthday, ten years before Áine and Patrick left Ireland. The trunk now cradled the clàrsach her grandson, Sean Michael Morgan, had made for his wife in 1896.

She climbed up into truck bed and lifted the trunk's lid. Even in the breezy morning air, she smelled the wildflowers, the scent of the earth, and sensed the memories and love it held.

Bright sunlight filled the trunk. Below the clàrsach, beneath the quilt, rested Yuri's balalaika. She hugged the instrument and then noticed the top of a book. Carefully lifting the fragile volume, she gently opened to the cover page and read, *Walden or Life in the Woods* by Henry D. Thoreau, 1854.

She smiled as tears gathered. Standing in the sun light, holding the book and the balalaika, she knew. *He'll be back.*

With the treasures safely stowed in the trunk, Morgan and Howard walked the labyrinth one last time. Sitting briefly on the bench at the center, she admired the pond, and listened to the natural spring water bubble over the rocks. "Thank you," she said in a soft voice.

She retrieved five carrots from the otherwise spotless, empty refrigerator before locking the back door for the last time. Starting the truck, she said goodbye to the dogwood tree then parked under the Douglas fir. The llamas seemed to understand. Howard watched from the passenger window as she broke off pieces of carrot and fed them. "Your new caretakers, the Reid's, will be here in the morning. They never had llamas before so you'll need to teach them like you taught me."

Leaning on the mammoth trunk of the Douglas fir, she looked up into its branches, and said softly, "I think I'll miss you most of all."

She stopped at the General Store in Port Gamble for a latte and warm cinnamon roll on the way to the cottage.

Her life began… once more.

Epilogue

*I went to the woods because I wished
to live deliberately, to front only
the essential facts of life, and see if
I could not learn what it had to teach,
and not, when I came to die,
discover that I had not lived."*

—Henry David Thoreau

ONLY NATURAL SOUNDS BROKE THE SILENCE at Morgan's beachside home, rather than man-made obstacles to thought. On the porch every morning, and evening, after meditation, she quietly played the clàrsach as if serenading the forest with her love. Her audience included four-footed and feathered guests who demanded nothing of her.

She hung a bird feeder filled with sunflower seeds, but before the chickadees, grosbeaks, or nuthatch arrived, a black bear tore it to bits. *I can't get much closer to nature than this*, she thought as she hosed bear scat from her well-worn Ugg boots.

High above the cottage, eagles floated effortlessly in the wind, singing as songbirds. The hummingbirds hunkered down for winter in a tall bush on Teekalet Bluff, making chipping sounds when Morgan and Howard came too close. When three inches of snow blanketed the porch, the Anna's Hummingbirds seemed grateful for the feeder filled with sugar water. Morgan photographed them hovering in mid-air and sitting in the snow and marveled that the tropical-looking little birds wintered near her cottage. During the long dark nights, the coyotes sang to her from the dense forest on either side of the yard. The rabbits hid all day, but when snow covered the grass, their three-pointed paw prints revealed their overnight visit.

Morgan and Howard walked the beach every day. At low tide, a base of colorful rocks and wet sand supported clam and cockleshells, bleached white and weathered fragile by the surf. Each crunchy step reminded Morgan of frozen snow in Ohio but the cool breeze smelled of seaweed, salt, and wood smoke. Humidity nourished her skin in weather that made *damp* a verb. She gathered pockets full of shells and smooth stones, glued them together in cairn-like stacks and sold them at a tourist shop in Port Gamble. Sometimes, overpowered by inspiration, Morgan wrote late at night and slept all morning. Howard waited good-naturedly.

Standing on the bluff in the dark, she watched shooting stars and listened to the north wind combine with high winter tides to produce metrical waves and the clicking percussion of small rocks as the saltwater receded. Then the tympani beat of the next wave.

If Morgan unplugged the telephone and turned off her computer, no synthetic sound disturbed her—just wind and water and calling eagles. Of course, an airplane could fly over, a fishing boat might pass, and the icemaker occasionally dropped its cache, but her solitude and inspiration remained uncompromised.

To someone living a hectic life of cooperation and compromise, her retreat seemed like an updated version of Thoreau's *Walden*. Surrounded by nature, dreams, and memories, she lived deliberately, learning to awaken to the world around her, unencumbered by irrelevant noise, demands, and conflict.

As Howard sniffed seaweed and oyster shells, she thought of Yuri, as she often did, and the nights they spent by the fire under the stars. She remembered their last walk in the tree farm and wondered if they would ever travel together on the astral plane as they did that last wondrous evening together.

December 22, 2012, marked the beginning of a new era as well as Yuri's fortieth birthday. She wanted to share this transitional day with him in some way.

She decided to build a big fire in the fireplace then call to wish him a happy birthday.

Climbing the steps from the beach, she noticed a familiar figure, like a hologram, standing on the porch. He hugged the clàrsach in one arm and the balalaika in the other.

Let's play our duet in the mountains.

Morgan and Howard settled into his red convertible. Her hair twisted in the wind as they traveled west on Highway 104. The snow-capped Olympic Mountains beckoned with fuchsia luminescence while a dazzling rainbow of light saturated the space between them.

the end

Author Biography

Once a globe-trotting corporate executive, Marcia Breece lives in a beach house in Port Townsend, Washington, where she enjoys the tranquility and solitude she needs to breathe deeply. The Strait of Juan de Fuca provides daily photo opportunities, whether it's the foggy beach at sunrise, bald eagles drifting on the wind, or dogs chasing salty waves. "My wanderlust has passed. This is what I need for now."

Writing became her outlet in the late 1970s when she began journaling. In the 1990s she wrote white papers, user manuals, and articles for technical magazines but longed to write what was in her heart. Meanwhile, she realized she couldn't breathe deeply enough and still show up at the office. A line from Mary Oliver's poem said it all: "…are you breathing just a little and calling it a life?" (Have You Ever Tried to Enter the Long Black Branches?) In 2005 she left the corporate world to buy a llama ranch, where she ran a bed and breakfast for five years. Although she managed to finish her memoir, Finding This Place, she found that farm chores and inn keeping left little time for writing. In 2011, she closed the inn, sold the farm, and found Port Townsend where she treasures the freedom to live an authentic life.

For more information, please visit her www.marciabreece.com.

Deruny

UKRAINIAN POTATO – APPLE PANCAKES RECIPE
12 to 18 pancakes

Ingredients
5-8 red potatoes
2 or 3 tart apples (Granny Smith work well)
1 large yellow onion
1 or 2 eggs
3 tablespoon flour or more if necessary
1 cup plain yogurt (or sour cream) for mixture, and garnish
salt and pepper to taste
lard or coconut oil

Method
Peel potatoes
Peel and core apples
Clean onion
Grate potatoes, apples and onion alternately into a large bowl, mixing as
you grate. (Onion juice prevents potatoes and apples from turning brown)
Add flour and egg
Add 1-2 tablespoons yogurt
Mix well with wooden spoon or your hands
Add salt and black pepper (about 1 teaspoon salt, ¼ teaspoon pepper)
Batter will be soupy enough to ladle easily (if too runny add more flour)
Heat griddle to high
Coat with lard or oil
Drop mixture one heaping tablespoon at a time
Fry on one side until golden brown before turning
Brown other side
Serve warm Deruny with cold yogurt garnish (or sour cream)

Membrillo
QUINCE PASTE RECIPE
*A sweet spread or paste made from quince that
can be sliced and spread on toast or used as pastry filling.*

Ingredients
8 - 12 ripe quince (firm and bright yellow), washed,
peeled, cored, roughly chopped. Fruit is very firm.
1 tablespoon vanilla
Lemon zest from two lemons
3 tablespoon lemon juice
Equal parts quince puree and sugar ~ 4 cups of granulated sugar *(see below)*

Method
Place quince pieces in a heavy Dutch oven and cover with water (6-8 quarts)
Add lemon zest
Bring to a boil.
Reduce to simmer, cover, and let cook until quince is tender (about 40 min)
Allow to cool slightly (for safety's sake)
Strain the water from the quince pieces
Purée the quince pieces and lemon peel in a food processor, blender,
or food mill
Measure the quince purée and measure equal part sugar
(example: 4 cups of purée + 4 cups sugar)
Return the quince purée to the large pan
Heat to medium-low
Add sugar
Stir with a wooden spoon until the sugar has completely dissolved
Add lemon juice and vanilla
Continue to cook over low heat, stirring occasionally, for 1½ to 2 hours or more,
until very thick and very deep orange/red color

Preheat oven to a low 125°F (52°C)
Line a 9 x 12 baking pan with parchment paper
Grease parchment with butter
Pour quince paste into parchment-lined baking pan
Smooth out top of paste with buttered wooden spoon
Place in oven to dry, 1 – 2 hours or longer
When firm, remove from oven and let cool

Served sliced with Manchego cheese
Refrigerate membrillo wrapped in plastic wrap

Book Club Discussion Questions

1. Yuri and Morgan are very attracted to one another but romance and sexual intimacy are not part of their relationship. Why did the author decide to keep their relationship "nonphysical?"

2. How did the glasses help Morgan learn to love herself? What other growth/learning experiences happened as a result of finding the glasses?

3. What passages/vignettes strike you as insightful or profound?

4. Breece used wind and storms to symbolize change. List other examples of symbolism you noticed. How did symbolism influence the story?

5. Breece used several settings, primarily the llama farm, the tree farm, the caves, and the beach at the end. Why were the settings important to the story? Explain.

6. Did Breece develop realistic male and female characters?

7. Did places, objects, or animals become characters? Explain.

8. How were the secondary characters important to the story? Mr. Wakefield? Meredith? Biz? Ruth? Do the secondary characters grow or mature?

9. Who was your favorite character? Why?

10. In Chapter 15 a woman appears in the labyrinth. Who do you think she was?

    "Right after I found the glasses, a woman appeared like a shadowy hologram in the labyrinth. I felt as if she welcomed me to this land. The yellow wool shawl over her shoulders waved in the breeze and her long, narrow face had deeply weathered skin."

11. Although Morgan mentioned her daughter a number of times, the story did not include her. How did this make you feel? Why do you think Breece did this?

12. Describe the dynamics between Morgan and Biz. How does their relationship change?

13. How would you describe the changes in Morgan from the time she bought the farm until she moved to the cottage?

14. Was foreshadowing and suspense effective? Did Breece give away too much at the beginning of the book? Explain.

15. Has this novel changed you or broadened your perspective? Were you exposed to different ideas about people, religion, or spirituality?

16. Did the book end the way you expected? How?

17. If you could ask the author, Marcia Breece, a question, what would you ask?

Your questions and comments are appreciated.
Feel free to contact Marcia Breece at www.marciabreece.com/contact